In memory of
Elsbeth Marie von Streubel Lohse-Hopp
whose own Poppy
was forever too
far away

Nobody's Fault

"...a history, mystery, coming-of-age story that works...."
—*Flamingnet Reviews*

"...characters are well developed...voices are distinct...
plot moves easily...."
—*School Library Journal*

Other
BalonaBooks

Nobody's Fault
Surprises from the Earth and the Heart

Jonathan Pearce

Baloba Books
STOCKTON, CALIFORNIA

Nobody's Fault
Surprises from the Earth and the Heart

Copyright © 2006 by Jonathan Pearce
The BalonaBooks logo is a Registered Trademark.

10 9 8 7 6 5 4 3 2 1

Publisher's Cataloging-in-Publication Data

Pearce, Jonathan.
  Nobody's fault : surprises from the earth and the heart / Jonathan Pearce.

       p. ;   cm.   (alk paper)
      ISBN-13: 9780976547938
      ISBN-10: 0976547937

1. Gifted girls--Juvenile fiction. 2. Journalism, High school--Juvenile fiction. 3. Centenarians--Juvenile fiction. 4. San Francisco Earthquake, Calif., 1906--Juvenile Fiction.
5. Gifted persons--Fiction. 6. Journalism, School--Fiction. 7. Older people--Fiction. 8. Earthquakes--California--Fiction. I. Title.

PS3531.E22 N63 2005
813/ . 6/083   2005905510

The text of this book is set in Dutch 801; decoration in News Gothic MT
Printed in the United States of America

Editor: Jon Riis
Cover: Barbara Hodge
Book Design: Cass Timerman

Published by
BalonaBooks, PO Box 690106-0106, Stockton, California

References

Everett, Marshall. *The Complete Story of the San Francisco Earthquake,* (Chicago, Bible House, 1906).

Funston, Frederick. "How the Army Worked to Save San Francisco," *Cosmopolitan Magazine,* July 1906. <http://www.sfmuseum.net/1906/cosmo.html> (5 Mar. 1996)

Hansen, G., and E. Condon. *Denial of Disaster,* (San Francisco, Chronicle Press, 1989)

Lawson, Andrew C. *The California Earthquake of April 18, 1906. Report of the State Earthquake Investigation Commission, Carnegie Institution of Washington, 1908,* Pub. no. 87, vol I. Reprinted 1969

Wilson, Kate. *Earthquake: San Francisco, 1906.* (New York, Raintree Publishers, 1992)

Acknowledgments

Heartfelt thanks to the junior high and high school students who read *Nobody's Fault* in manuscript and provided useful criticism.

Special thanks to careful readers Beverly J. Holt, Amelia Gianelli Cutler, and Thomas C. McKenzie. Each provided valuable commentary.

A splendid treasure of information about the Great San Francisco Quake and Fire of 1906 lies on the Internet, especially at <http://www.sfmuseum.net>

Prologue

The dream was pulling me into a shivery cold room, a place featuring a snake's nest of plastic tubes and the rhythmic clacking of a life-support machine. The especially loud click that my Korndog Klock emits every morning precisely at 3:30 woke me again and rescued me.

So I shivered off my futon and padded barefoot down the hall to Daddy's room, a usually warm place redolent of Old Spice. I crawled into his bed and sought heat, snuggling the length of my body next to his, the way I used to do when I was little and Mommy was still with us.

Daddy was lying on his back making little clicking snorts, not unlike my favorite movie dolphin Flipper. I slipped my arm across his bare chest in order to get my head close to his.

"It's okay, Daddy," I whispered into his ear. "It's only me." He stopped breathing.

He was quiet for a long time, but his heart was about to pound right up through my arm.

Probably he thought I was Mommy.

Then he said into the dark, "I think maybe you ought to go back to bed, Tery. We can have a talk tomorrow." And he turned over so his back was toward me. I felt sad right away, but I did what he said, not cold any more, but also mostly counting Korndog Klock clicks for the rest of the night.

We never did have that talk the next day. He still calls me Baby once in a while but, as if I might have some kind of skin disease he's afraid of, he doesn't hug me. I don't go into his bedroom any more, especially now that Penny's moved in and everything has changed.

Mommy won't explain Daddy's frosty attitude. "You'll figure it out some day," is all she'll say. I've figured out two or three explanations, none of which could possibly be, given Daddy's character.

But today Daddy got me started thinking also about some other things. I was practicing the piano part to the Schubert song cycle I'm learning. Daddy leaned against our new piano and looked at my hands moving on the keyboard.

I think that Mommy had somehow clued me as to the question he was going to ask. "You're still okay with the marriage, Tery?"

My handsome daddy hunk and Penny, his pretty new wife, can't seem to keep their hands off each other. It's sort of disturbing for Daddy's twelve-year-old daughter to watch, so I look the other way, try to think about other things.

"Sure. Okay," I said, taking my hands off the keyboard. "No problem. You asked Jack and me before, and we both said it was fine with us." I was not looking directly at him, but instead examining my fingernails that I keep, like his, clean and cut short.

2

His fine eyebrows down in a frown, Daddy said, "It's just that it seems to me you're staying a little distant from my Penny."

My Penny. That hurt. "It's just that it's still all sort of new, her being here." I was tempted to add: *and Mommy* not *being here.* Given that Mommy's terrible departure was more than seven years ago, I overcame that temptation. It wouldn't be a fair thing to say.

Daddy was a widower too long. Balona women, single and married, have remarked on that fact for years, all the while while pushing marriageable women at him, inviting him to "socials," dropping off casseroles "for the family," having romantic oldies dedicated to "the beautiful widower of Balona" as he was famously known on Delta City's KDC-FM.

I accepted the second marriage, and Daddy smiled, seemed satisfied, so enough said about that. But since I mentioned Penny's being new in our house, I thought I should add something to sort of send Daddy's worry to a final resting place. "And I like Claire a lot. Too."

Claire is the new wife's daughter, so she is now my smart and beautiful seventeen-year-old sister. Both of these women have recently become rich through inheritance — super-rich in Claire's case — a nice situation for Daddy who has always watched every nickel, dime, and now Penny, with great care. But the point Daddy finally raised wasn't about Penny and the wedding after all. I guess Daddy takes my loyalty for granted.

The question he came to was about community service and no idle hands for Tery. He said, "Y'know, Tery, because I'm now a school board member, me and Penny just gave a goodly sum to Balona High."

3

"Daddy, now that you're a school board member, you should say, 'Penny and I'."

Daddy's face turned not quite cerise. He lowered himself down onto the nearest couch, making the soft leather cushions sigh loudly. He lay back. "Well," he said. Daddy is a professional photographer and a sculptor with multiple awards. Although he's a university grad, and although his father is a legal scholar and his mother a concert pianist who speaks several languages, Daddy often reminds me that he's an academic product of the 1970s and 1980s, so he doesn't pay attention to grammar. I do, of course.

"Well, okay," he said. "Penny and I then. We've donated to pay for reviving the *Korndogger* for summer school over there. I want to see the paper get to be like it used to be."

"Good idea," I said, playing a major chord with both hands, hoping that I sounded enthusiastic. "It needs some reviving." The *Korndogger* should read like a high school paper, not like an exercise by little kids.

"Joaquin tells me you could get a summer gig there as sort of a foreign correspondent from Little Baloney." Daddy was referring to Mr. Joaquin Peralta, a long-time friend of his who teaches at Balona High School.

"At the high school? I'm not even old enough to be there, Daddy. I'm still a fixture at Little Baloney."

I put a minor third into the chord and made a *glissando*. I do think I'm a good writer, but high school? Not likely.

Daddy shook his head. "No, you have the talent. And me...Penny and I specifically earmarked the donation for the *Korndogger*. Penny remembered that I worked on it when I was a student back in the dark ages and still work for a newspaper." He laughed. He has bright, even teeth, a *Gentleman's Quarterly* smile to delight any dentist. But he doesn't smile often. Maybe I inherited that characteristic. "That means you got some connections there already."

"I've been thinking Claire might need some help, and I've already volunteered." By that I meant assisting at Claire's new enterprise on Front Street, her cybercafé.

He said, "Well, no reason you can't do that, too. But Joaquin says you could maybe write a feature story."

"I'd rather help Claire, Daddy. Have you committed me already?"

"No." He sighed. "Well, you can do whatever you want."

I plunked a few keys randomly, not to be recalcitrant, only to suggest that I was in the middle of something musical, and making room for him. He hasn't shot hoops with me for a long time.

Daddy went on. "But we just thought since you're talented enough to do just about anything, this would be a way to help out over there. Community service? And maybe you could be enough of a help in getting their one summer issue out to help get the paper revived full time. You would be demonstrating our family interest, too."

He scratched his chin. "In fact, it would be a big favor to me and Penny, Penny and I."

"Penny and me." Daddy looked surprised, but I went on. "Well, I'm not a journalist type. I'm a philosopher type. I'd rather think about something than write a newspaper story about it." I sighed, maybe dramatically.

"But all right, I'll try to help resurrect the *Korndogger*." Daddy smiled and nodded. I said, "Do they expect me to bring a junior high-type story with me?"

"You could call the young woman at this number to set up the appointment for interview. Sheba, he said her name is." Daddy stood up, reached into a back pocket of his

Levi's for his little notebook, and tore a page out for me. "Joaquin says this Sheba is maybe sort of hard to take, so watch out." Daddy frowned at himself. "Maybe I shouldn't have said that."

"Well, then, it's not a done deal," I said.

"Oh, no, it's something you have to qualify for."

"So who knows if I can do it?"

But Daddy smiled again, nodded, and went out humming, probably to give Penny a hug and tell her the good news.

People accuse me of being super-organized. I don't know about that. I'm aware that kids at school can't be exactly thrilled when a sort of obsessive, vocabulary-afflicted classmate also seems super-organized, so I try never to show off, not be seen as a know-it-all, as Jack keeps warning me about.

But I was born self-confident and with all kinds of abilities I don't have to work at, abilities that simply pop up at odd times, even without prodding from Senta Shaw, the great tutor Daddy hired for me when he caught me doing Jack's geometry problems (when I was in third grade). Senta, who is Sal's mom, is also giving me French lessons. I do have some talents that nobody else has. I don't know if journalism is one of them. I do know that I am blessed.

Except, I wish Daddy still loved me.

1

I am trying to get into a newspaper reporter mood

Seated again at our beautiful new Bösendorfer, I am still at work learning both the words and music to this Schubert song. My hands are in training to achieve a quiet, stable rhythm, while neighbor Richie Kuhl throws something against the side of our house, *bonk, bonk,* not at all in time with my rhythm.

The irritant of choice is probably one of my brother's expensive tennis balls that Richie surely stole from the storage shed in our backyard. If I open the window and yell at him to stop, he'll only say something obscene and continue his annoying behavior.

Or else he'll throw the ball at me. As his mother is in jail and his father and brother are both incompetent to control him, experience tells me that Richie will do whatever he wants.

If Jack were home instead of at summer school in Berkeley, I'd complain to him, and Jack would set Richie straight. Jack and I are communicating nowadays mostly by e-mail, so I can complain to him, at least to get frustration and irritation out of my throat where they usually park and cause me to cough like my grandpa. Irritation also sets my foot to tapping involuntarily, like a horse with thrush.

But the bumping against the house now ceases and is replaced by a clanking and mechanical coughing in the next-door driveway. Richie has evidently started his new motorcycle. He stole the machine in Delta City, according to local gossip.

In a moment Richie will probably be off to do some evil. It's unfortunate but necessary that I'll have to mention him repeatedly.

Yes, he is gone for now, and I close the book on its easel, sit up straight, close my eyes, and review the words and music that I have just memorized. German is not an easy language to sing, unless you're a German, and maybe not even then.

Besides, the only person around here who might really crave to hear me sing a German art song is Obahchan, my Japanese granny. A multi-linguist, she will be able to correct any mispronunciations. I am determined to play and sing the entire group of songs and surprise not only Obahchan but also Jack, whose piano playing is virtuoso quality. I might also surprise my new sister Claire who can both tootle her flute and pound nicely on the piano.

"For a pessimist, you sure are a quick study," Jack complains to me a hundred times a week. Right now he's deep into anatomy, a subject even he finds to be a challenge. Jack tells me I ought to go around singing "Tomorrow" from the musical *Annie.*

Lighten up, he says.

Don't be such a worrywart, he says. Jack's opinion puzzles me. I am an optimist.

Grandpa lives next door and is another one who tells me not to take the world and its problems so seriously. He also tells me all the time, "Enjoy that brain of yours while you can, Tery. Entropy is always creeping up." Grandpa, a big man with a blond beard turning white, jokes like that. People have said that I joke like him. But what he has said is scientific fact. I worry a bit about having these special gifts, not to speak of a vocabulary that grows heavier every day and that must surely annoy even my teachers.

To offer a small brag about my memory, I have as of this moment three songs already learned, words and music, vocal and piano, after only a couple days of work, seven songs more to learn in the cycle. Jack is probably wagging his head and wrinkling his lips in mock envy at this very moment.

So I decide to quit for the morning, feeling already successful. Although I have not quite conquered Schubert, Richie's arhythmic intrusions have not defeated me. I count that a victory.

I waltz from the hugely expensive new baby grand that Penny has given us to one of the new couches Penny has also bought for her acquired family. I sprawl across the noisy cushions, comfy in the loose blue scrubs I like to wear around the house in warm weather.

Penny seems to have sprayed the area with something fragrant, or maybe it's her own faint scent that's nowadays everywhere in our house, sort of a hint of vanilla and nutmeg.

If I had bought into the latest of the many golden rumors that went around school just before we quit for vacation, I would believe that becoming a teenager and thus departing childhood will make me automatically cool and mature. At any rate, I still have a long way to go, as we blew out the candles on my most recent cake back in gray February. A long way yet to go, as it's now only yellow-green June in beautiful Balona, CA 95232.

I lie back, watch shrub shadows breeze-moved on the ceiling, and consider again Daddy's suggestion that I call a girl named Sheba. Hard-to-take Sheba, he said. She's only a high school kid. High school kids can't be *that* hard to take. On the other hand, Richie Kuhl is a high school student, when he deigns to attend.

So now I have a few more summer goals to work on. First, I'll have to learn the rest of the song cycle. Second, I need to do what I can to help those Balona High School kids make Daddy's *Korndogger* project a reality and a success.

2

Interview at Balona High School surprises newbie reporter

The condition of the person sprawled on the classroom floor is not one of the actual horrors that I'll encounter in the next couple of weeks. However, her position and appearance are both unpleasant and unexpected. She is lying on her back, one knee up, her hand over her mouth, eyes rolling. It is hard to see all of her or hear what she is saying because of the high school students clustered around her, all talking at once.

"It was her stupid boyfriend smacked her. Richie Kuhl hit Sheba." I do know quite a few high school kids through Jack, but this comment is from a dark-haired girl I don't know.

"Serves her right," and words to that effect mumbled by several. Sheba, who is to be my interviewer, is the floored victim.

A minute ago, as I tried to enter for my *Korndogger* interview, I was bumped aside by a figure in a gray hooded sweatshirt dashing out of the classroom door. That person gave off a ripe smell, like a korndog left in a lunchbag over a long vacation. The odor remaining is in fact redolent of Richie Kuhl, my aforementioned neighbor who not only bounces things off our house and steals motorcycles, but is reputed also to torture small animals, throw dirt clods at elderly people, and sell acid stamps to elementary kids, according to just about anybody you might ask.

"Well, I bet it's back to the Runcible Hall of Fame for Richie Kuhl." This from Mr. Croon, Principal of Balona High, growling over my shoulder. He, too, now is pushing me aside, growling, "Where'd Joaquin go to now? Where's your teacher?" The circle of the crowd gives way.

"Mister Peralta's right here." The resonant baritone voice comes from the man with the cup of water and the paper towel, now kneeling next to the figure on the floor.

"You'll be able to tell who I am right away since I dress like a fashionable lady, not like your usual Balona tramp," Sheba Weiner had remarked to me after we identified ourselves on the phone last night. The ladylike dress is now bunched unfashionably. Sheba is snuffling into Mr. Peralta's paper towel.

Both of Sheba's knees are now up, pink-flowered underpants are prominent. A bare expanse of pale abdominal flesh is also on display. "All right now?" he asks.

"I'm gonna get him," she says through her fingers. "Him and his jailbird mama both." Sheba is probably referring to the fact that Richie Kuhl's mother, Mrs. Bapsie Kuhl, infamous in our town, was only yesterday taken off to the Chaud County jail in Delta City by her own brother, Sheriff Anson Chaud, and is now "waiting on raiment, eksedra," as the sheriff describes such things.

He is not known as an intellectual.

Mr. Peralta helps Sheba to her feet. "I thought you were rescuing Richie from a life of crime, Sheba. What brought on the violence?"

Sheba sways, holding her head, gropes her way across the room where she sags into a chair.

I have seen much older women, Daughters of the Delta, display the same operatic behavior, the weight of great tragedy on their shoulders, practically *La Traviata*.

"What brought it on?" Sheba wails. "What brought it on? I called him up and like told him to come over and get featured in a interview and then we could go up to Front Street and have korndogs together." Mr. Peralta's eyebrows twitch upwards. "Or maybe tacos. We could have tacos together, and Richie could buy for a change. He's off his meds, y'know." She bites her lip. "I shouldn't mention that part. Anyways, he showed up just before you got here."

Sheba seems to be accusing Mr. Peralta of somehow promoting Richie's assault. She continues. "And then I like started off my nice interview by just asking him a simple nice question about his ma is all. So?"

Sheba sniffs.

"Well, Sheba, that would set Richie off, especially with his mother in jail, and especially if you used that tone of voice." It's evident from Mr. Peralta's statement that he doesn't approve of Sheba's manner, a combination of sneer and whine. "Anyway, we won't see more of him this summer, I bet."

"You lookin' at me, kid?" This is from frowning Sheba. I am standing in the middle of the room and realize I have been not quite amused, but certainly staring. "I'm here about the correspondent job? We talked about it last night? Phone? I'm Tery Ordway."

"Oh. The child genius from Little Baloney." The other students all glance from their work. Sheba scowls and looks me up and down. "They say you got the highest IQ in the USA, maybe the world. That true?"

I laugh. "I don't know about that." If you're supposed to be smart, people expect you to know everything. I don't know everything. Sheba makes a mouth, glossed geranium-red lower lip stuck out, corners turned down.

Mr. Peralta takes over, introduces me to each member of the group of seven journalists present. "Tim Runcible's sports," he says of a serious-looking boy wearing gold-rim glasses. I smile around, don't pay too much attention to the rest of the introductions.

Tim is nicest looking, lips like those on a classic statue. Reminds me of Daddy, except blond. A lot older than I, of course. Quiet looking.

I tend to absorb, rather than listen carefully. Bad habit for a would-be reporter. But I know I'll be able to recall all the names later—and what each was wearing and the sound of each voice, color of their eyes. I am blessed with that kind of memory so my head is full of details. Mommy calls it's a blessing. Sometimes I wonder.

Sheba resumes the assessment. "Well, you're tall enough so you'd maybe pass for about fifteen or so, except it looks like you got no boobs." Sheba sniffs.

Individuals watching from desks and tables laugh, but not unkindly. I nod and chuckle, showing that I can take a jab without getting upset. And I know that female breast-size is inordinately important to many males and females in our small town. I can wait for my enlargements without anxiety. If they never grow into show pieces, I can stand that, too, as Mommy tells me they sometimes get in the way and can be bothersome.

Mr. Peralta smiles. "We don't have much time this afternoon since I've got to rush up to TacoTime before the noon rush is all over, so perhaps we could get right to work and give Tery her first assignment." He says this with a question implied, but Sheba appears not to be listening to him.

"You got any journalism experience at all, kid?" Sheba, evidently now recovered, sticks a pencil in the dark-blonde curls over her ear, shuffles some papers, appears busy, executive, editorial.

"None at all. But I'll do my best. I have some ideas for features."

"Oooooh no you don't. I'm the one gives assignments, so I'm the one tells you what stories to write. Try to write. First we got to see if you got enough grammar, eksedra."

Mr. Peralta intervenes from his desk, only a couple of feet away. "Tery's already demonstrated her writing ability to her teachers, Sheba. She's ready to go now."

"Well, if I'm gonna be in charge of this paper, I guess I can make the decision what subordinates get to be on my junior staff." Sheba speaks in the typically loud Balona female voice. In a smaller voice she adds: "But all right. I guess this is all politics anyways."

Mr. Peralta smiles. "Mmm-hmm," he says.

It seems to me he is trying not to roll his eyes. He asks, "How's your lip? Feeling a little better?"

"I'm thinking about hiring Mr. Burnross to sue that blorp. That bleep. Richie's my boyfriend, y'know. He told me he likes me. Boys. God." She moves her lips variously, testing them, finally looks at me. "C'mon over here and set and let me like give you an assignmcnt, sort of try you out. We don't got much time, y'know, what with only four weeks for summer school, and now only two weeks left of

15

that. You should've showed up here a couple weeks ago."
Sheba grunts her dissatisfaction. "Well, never mind. Takes
all kinds. And we like got practically no budget, since that
dumb school board won't give us any money."

She gives me a scornful look, although Daddy's and
Penny's donation was the lead story in our twice-weekly
community paper, the Balona *Courier,* just this week. My
toe taps four or five times spontaneously and I cough.

"So I got it figured you're like sort of a junior shirttail
relative of mine, y'know. You look surprised. Through
Claire. Yeah, she's the shirttail. Yeah. Claire's like probably my second cousin, according to Pastor Nim, who's
also maybe a second cousin. He told me that I might con-
nect to a lot of guys through old Pastor Preene. He was a
sex fiend, y'know, Pastor Preene was."

Sheba sniffs, rubs her nose, leans toward me, frowning.

"I'm talking Pastor Preene here, not Pastor Nim, remember. It was Pastor Preene made out with my mother while
she was like still married to Reuben Fring, probably." She
tosses her head. "My little brother's probably got more
Preene blood than I have, but. Just look at him some time.
His actual name is Pius, y'know, like old Pastor Preene
himself, but everybody's always called him Pee, since, well,
you know."

She leans back in her chair, gestures broadly with her
thumb and hip to illustrate Pee at work, perhaps trying for
distance, as boys are said to do. She laughs and claps her
hands at her own performance.

"I know Pee," I confess. "He's my classmate. He looks a
lot like Zachary Burnross."

"Zack. Well, see, that's my point: Old Pastor Preene, sex
fiend. Got around. 'Nuff said." Sheba sniffs, perhaps for
emphasis. Her sniffing is becoming predictable.

16

I find Sheba's facts and opinions interesting and repulsive, like gossip generally, but keep my expression neutral, as a competent journalist should.

I decide not to remind Sheba that I'm related to my new sister Claire not by blood, but only by my daddy's marriage to Penny, so Sheba's *shirttail* is quite accurate. I'm glad I have both mother and father again. Two mothers, in fact: one real to me, but one that some people would call a figment; the recent one nice enough, but possibly a temp.

Who knows about relationships nowadays? I don't tell Sheba that my objective here is simply to do the best job I can and impress my daddy who doesn't seem to like me as much as he used to.

I say, "So maybe you really ought to be the one to do this article, since you know all the dirt on everybody."

She frowns again. "I give the orders, kid. Just remember that." She squints at my legs. "They say kids like you, even though you make everybody uncomfortable since you talk so funny and wear those dumb stockings. "They say you're a favorite weird person down at Little Baloney. That true?"

"I guess we'll find out, sooner or later." I try not to sound flip. I know that Richie Kuhl doesn't like me. It's probably not true that everybody else does like me. It doesn't matter; I don't really care whether they do or don't. It's news to me that I talk funny. I do like puns and I tell jokes that I think are funny, but my humor doesn't always comport with that of my classmates, many of whom still prefer fart jokes to anything subtle. Maybe that's what Sheba means. I do try to use appropriate words.

Sheba sniffs. "Well, I'm not so easy to, like, get over on. So it's just that like now I got this off of my chest, so you know not to mess with me."

"Wouldn't dream of it," I say.

"You're looking at my hair? I got like bugs up there?"

"It's probably the expression my face gets when I'm thinking. I tend to look upwards."

"Uh-huh. And you sure don't talk or act like you're only twelve."

"I don't act at all. What you see is what's inside." I am not being entirely open here. I am fully aware of some advantages I have that I'd certainly not discuss with a person who has a dark-red aura that sizzles.

"Well, we'll see. Long as you don't try to crowd me."

The high school classroom smells different from my Little Baloney classrooms. "Little Baloney" is what we kids call our junior high. Of course Balona High is "Big Baloney."

The chalk smell here is the same, and the heat of the early summer afternoon is beginning to pound through the single-pane windows the same. The major difference is the human smell, not quite repulsive, but definitely not a little-kid smell and definitely not like orange blossoms or clean sheets.

I try to be less frosty. "Your bracelet is engraved BW."

"Well, you do got good eyes." She holds up the bracelet. "Yeah, well, that's for my full name. Bathsheba, not just the Sheba part, but like in the Bible? Probably I got Biblical Runcible relatives." Sheba doesn't have to explain, for every Balonan knows that the Biblical Runcibles name their offspring after Bible characters, whereas the Vegetable Runcible branch name their kids after plants. Tim Runcible's given name surely is Timothy. It could represent either branch.

Sheba's eyes squint. "Somebody said you do karate. Is that actual or fictual?"

"I play tennis and sail and ride horses with my brother and his friends. They're all big guys and beat me at most stuff. I don't do karate."

I don't mention my five years of aikido study and my striving for black belt competence.

Sheba is obviously "getting to know" me, but I decide I could use some psychology to move the discussion along, so I try a technique my wicked but lovable Uncle Jess always brags about using.

"Well, Sheba," I say, "You've really taken charge over here, and you show plenty of style. I think I'll like working for you. So I guess the *Korndogger* will win some sort of prize, if we junior staff all do our share for you."

Sheba does have a style and she has taken charge, so those observations are true, if a bit forced. Sheba glows, sits back, breathes. "What? Well. Yeah, you got that right, all right. Yeah. Well, you said you like had an idear about a story? That what you said?"

"My grandpa was talking about old folks around town, and I thought…"

"Ooooh no." Sheba shudders. "Old folks got no sex value. Total un-meg. Kids want kid stuff. Kids got sex value."

I explain, "I was thinking about getting an old person to talk about the kind of kid stuff that my grandpa tells me was important in the old days. Maybe even something that kids nowadays would find interesting."

"Old folks playing Bingo. Wow. More un-meg, yo. No kid wants to read about old folks's thrills. Besides, wait till you like have Mr. Drumhandler's class. We get enough old folk's history in class."

She sniffs. Apparently there's no pleasing Sheba. I cough and my toe makes four or five rather loud taps on the vinyl tile floor, but for no reason obvious to Sheba. She peers under the table and then looks at me as if I were Moe Stooge who's just done something incomprehensible.

"You got a flea, I guess," she remarks.

I take a breath, recover my center.

I say, "Parents of kids might like to read one story about old folks's kid stuff. And they might get to talking about how cool the *Korndogger* has become under your leadership, now that it's interesting not only for kids, but parents, too."

She narrows her eyes and her lips twist. "Where'd you learn to talk like that? I mean, really, you sound like you're thirty years old. You talk like Dr. Thrust, only maybe not quite so phony-sounding."

Dr. Thrust is our school superintendent, who speaks always as if he's disclosing top-secret confidences.

"I don't know. We speak like this at home. Like we're talking now, one intelligent person to another."

One side of Sheba's lip comes up again, her almost-smile. "Figgers. You talk just like Jack." She sniffs.

Jack is a recent Balona High valedictorian. The other straight-A grad is my new sister, Claire.

Sheba shakes her head. "So, you like got a couple old geezers all lined up, have you?"

"Not yet, but I could make a list of possibles. Maybe more than one has an exciting tale to tell."

"Just remember who's in charge." Sheba pokes her finger into an imaginary eyeball. "I can spike your story any time I want. You know what it means to us journalists?"

"Spike. Does it mean cancel?"

"Yeah. If I don't like it, your story's toast." She sniffs.

Mr. Peralta has been listening to all this. "Well, Sheba, it's true that you're in charge, so you'll need to stay on top of this story of Tery's, whatever it is, so that we all profit from your expertise." Mr. Peralta does not sound sarcastic. I get the feeling that he wants or maybe even *needs* for Sheba to be successful. Maybe she's been forced on him.

"Well, I'll do my best." I sound like I'm groveling.

"So, Sheba, it seems to me that you've about made your decision to approve Tery's choice of subject?" Mr. Peralta is using much the same psychology I have been using: Don't act superior. Direct your attention to the other person's hoped-for self-image and address it respectfully.

I have found it to be a very effective technique. Not dishonorably manipulative. People like to feel respected and useful. Most people want to be seen as respected and competent, even if they're snippy and crabby and self-centered and irritable and bossy. When you give them the opportunity to be decent, they will usually come through. That's what my daddy says, and Grandpa and Obahchan. Mommy says so, too, but since she's no longer alive in the generally accepted sense, I have to interpret her intention.

"Made my decision. Yeah, I guess," says Sheba, looking satisfied.

Well, I've had my interview and been hired for the job. Now it remains for me to do whatever it takes to get the job done.

Maybe then I can get Daddy on my side again.

3

Cub reporter begins
search for subject

"I wish he'd make up his mind about who's really actually running this thing," Sheba remarks, popping her gum, and talking about Mr. Peralta who sits smiling, probably continuing to observe our interaction. "My dad is Sidney Weiner, step-dad actually, if you have to know. He's like pretty powerful on the faculty, y'know. He's good friends with Ms. Frackle, the head of the teachers' union, and what she says, like, goes." Sheba glosses the new black lipstick she is applying during our conversation.

Maybe it's dark green.

Mr. Peralta has been listening. "I think both Ms. Frackle and Mr. Weiner are influential people in our organization. But it was Mr. Croon who suggested that Sheba here might make a fine editor-in-chief. I'm happy the principal recommended her."

"He's happy I got the editor job, since it like gives him some cash for the summer."

Sheba is referring not to Principal Croon, but to Mr. Peralta as if he were not even present. Sheba's manner of speech renders what she says somehow insulting to hear aloud.

My foot twitches itself again. I cough briefly.

"You'll do a fine job, Sheba." Mr. Peralta nods to himself and looks at papers in a folder. He's probably used to Sheba's peculiarities. He continues to monitor our conference, and Sheba continues with her instructions.

She speaks between bites at a cuticle. "Now that I like thought some about it, you can go ahead and like interview anybody — anybody interesting. I mean, I don't mind you finding like some old guy, long as he's had some excitement in his life." Sheba points at me. "Of course, you got to write it up so it sounds exciting, not like world class Bingo over there at the Jolly Times. But first off, you really ought to like see this guy I got connections with."

Sheba suddenly smiles, lifts her chin at Mr. Peralta who appears not to be paying attention. "Some people think I don't got any brains or guts, either one." She tosses her head. "Hah. I'm a junior here now, y'know, not a freshman. A mature person. I even got a philosophy of life, y'know. And I got plenty of guts."

I hear giggling from a nearby table. Evidently, our classmates are listening.

Sheba then tells me about her "friend of the family," Mr. Q.Z. Wonkerly, a key employee at King Korndog. "I can get you the interview. He likes me. Mr. Q.Z. Wonkerly's wife's name is Sheba, too. I sort of showed him I wasn't wimpy about it, y'know. That was when me and Richie was still speaking the other day, and he took me over there to King Korndog Inkorporated to check out the action."

Sheba frowns. "Actually, I would say that Richie is pretty brave, when you get right down to it."

I ask, "Mr. Q.Z. Wonkerly said you weren't wimpy. What weren't you wimpy about?"

"Well, I wasn't scared to watch Richie do it. I got right up close when he did it. Mr. Q.Z. Wonkerly said out loud that I could probably do it, too."

"You made a korndog."

"No, no. It was Richie grabbed that thing they got over there at King Korndog, in the back of the place, y'know, the thing with the air hose on one end and the thing on the other?" Sheba gets up and demonstrates with gestures. "And he like went right over where they had this sheep looking at me, and he stuck the thing-part on the top of the sheep's head, back here, like Mr. Q.Z. Wonkerly showed us, and he went and like squeezed the trigger and *whish-bonk*, down went that dumb sheep. 'Whee.' Richie went, and they grappled his legs and chained him up and *whish-clank-zoom,* up he went and like sailed off on the rail, y'know, to get his throat cut, eksedra."

Sheba pauses, thinks, explains. "The sheep, that is. It was like cool, except for the wet turds he let all over the floor. Mr. Q.Z. Wonkerly said Richie could be his assistant any time. Richie took right to it."

"Mr. Q.Z. Wonkerly is one of the slaughterers over at King Korndog?"

"Chief Stunker is what they call him. They got other guys who can stunk, too, but he does it best. And quick. You wouldn't believe how many he can do in just a few minutes. So fast they got to tell him to like slow down till they can catch up over to where they cut and gut. That's how they say it: Cut and gut." Sheba is breathing heavily, her cheeks suddenly pink, her eyes shining. "For pigs, he said they do it some different. They like stick the thing here on the front of the pig's head instead of on the top. Mr. Q.Z. Wonkerly says that with sheep they got to stick it on top of the sheep's head, y'know, back right here?" Sheba indicates with her thumb the precise location. "On account of the front's got like too much bone there, only they didn't have a pig for Richie to demonstrate on for me, y'know. Oh, and they use a different thing to put down cows. Like bigger and stronger, y'know. Mr. Sly himself told me that. He owns the whole place, y'know. He was standing right there watching me and Richie."

Mr. Peralta rouses himself from his papers. "Seems to me, Sheba, that what with your excellent contacts and having had that experience, maybe you could be the one to write a prize-winning story about the background of a King Korndog." Mr. Peralta looks at the ceiling. "Hmm. You could make your headline something like, Reporter Witnesses Stunning Experience." Laughter from Tim and a couple other kids.

"Yeah. Well, I think you mean *editor* witnesses, eksedra. But I was just letting the kid here know that her editor-in-chief's got like contacts, y'know." She frowns. "But however, yeah. Good idear. I'll assign that story to myself, kid, since it's sort of in line with my philosophy of life. And you can do whatever you want, providing you clear it with me." She sniffs.

Sheba shakes her bracelet and looks at her wristwatch. "Actually, I could probably like forgive Richie, since he's so brave, eksedra. He's got a hot spirit, y'know, and I did sort of insult the memory of his mother. Well, my hot lunch date's ran off, but I still got a social fabric I got to see to right now, so I'm like out of here." She picks up papers and marches out in her short-step elderly way. I can visualize Sheba, stout at fifty, as a Daughter of the Delta, in a puce robe, marching around Veterans Hall. Several of the staff members perform a choral sniff after her exit. I'm wondering how Sheba got to be editor.

"Now, now," says Mr. Peralta, not exactly smiling.

So we have finally agreed — Mr. Peralta acting as intermediary and my quiet advocate — that I might think about whom to interview, and then make my selection without needing to check back with Sheba.

Mr. Peralta at last puts down his folder, looks out the window, suggests that I do try to get to somebody interesting to interview. He sighs, looks at the ceiling, and suggests again that I clear my selection with Sheba anyway, "just to make her feel better." I don't ask him to define interesting, but I take it to mean unusual.

I ask him, "Do you have any suggestions, Mr. Peralta?"

"No, I don't. That's the beauty of being an investigative reporter, Tery. You'll work with your editor, and I'll be happy to advise from time to time, but the best part of the job is that you get to make your own choices as to subject."

"Well, there are plenty of interesting subjects in Balona. I guess it'll take me some time to figure out."

"Except that you have only this week," he says. "After that, the paper must be all planned."

He's giving me a deadline, something I already know about. So, even as I say goodbye to Mr. Peralta and the couple of kids still in the room, I begin thinking about whom to interview.

First thought produces our neighbor, Mr. Kenworth Kuhl — he's Richie's and Joseph's father — is odd and very interesting. The latest rumor is that Mr. Kenworth

Kuhl's concussion won't keep him in the hospital much longer, so when he comes home, he'd be convenient to interview.

But although Mr. Kenworth Kuhl was a soldier and is reputed to be a great shot with a pistol, a stellar recommendation around Balona, he is also sort of generally lost-headed, what with his magpie intruding. He sees this magpie in all sorts of places, but almost nobody else sees it. At first you think he's joking when he tells you about it and points at it. No, he's serious, but then you look closely, trying to see it where he's pointing. He becomes worried that you don't see it, too.

Daddy says Mr. Kenworth Kuhl is "troubled" and that troubled people are more likely than other folks to see strange sights. I guess so. I think I'd be troubled, too, if I were married to Mrs. Kuhl. But she's "somebody interesting," too, now being in the Delta City jail. She'll probably be charged with battery or spousal abuse or both, and so is not really convenient to interview.

I could interview my grandpa, retired judge Alexander Ordway, as an Old Folk. Maybe I could get him to tell me a war story. No. Jack once asked him to do that, and Grandpa closed his eyes, shook his head. "Been there, done that," Grandpa said.

I could get Obahchan, my grandmother, to tell me about her experiences at home in Japan as a girl. But those experiences I've heard all my life sound very "usual," like experiences I myself had as a child right here in Balona. Obahchan talks about her own grandma and her grandma's garden. Different were the foods they ate and how they heated the house in winter and their sleeping arrangements. They don't seem "unusual" to me any more. They were really very different from my own experiences, but they became so familiar that I got used to them. Sushi and sukiyaki are as common to me as shredded wheat and apple pie. Perhaps I am more of an anomaly than I had thought.

While walking home, I admire all the beautiful front-yard flower plantings our citizens are so proud of, but as I round our corner, there is Richie Kuhl, crouching among the dandelions and crabgrass of his overgrown lawn, apparently trying to zero-in on Zachary Burnross across the street with something flung from Richie's slingshot. Zachary is a cute seventeen-year-old with glasses and very red hair of the same color as the hair of my daddy's beautiful new wife. Zachary lives down the block across the street.

He is trying to cut Mrs. Pezmyer's lawn with his push-mower while shouting that he's going to get his father to sue if Richie doesn't cut it out.

Zachary's father is Kenworth Burnross, a lawyer infamous for suing neighbors.

When Richie sees me, he shifts his position as if he might be about to fling something at me with his little boy's weapon. I can now see what he's been firing: small purple plums.

Richie's aura is almost the same as Balona summer lawn color, green-yellow. It sizzles.

"No, Richie," I say in a good strong voice. "If you fire that at me, I'll have to come after you and defend myself."

He scowls, stuffs his slingshot in his back pocket, says a rude word. Then stops short, turns toward me. "You Ordways are always picking on me. You sure don't know nothing about me. You don't know what I got to put up with." It looks like he has tears in his eyes. I've never seen this before in Richie Kuhl, a kid who was Jack's classmate for years, until he flunked too often. All at once I feel a lump in my throat for a kid with a mean mother and a disturbed father.

Then his expression changes. He smirks. "You guys found Claire's cat yet?" Claire's beautiful new Siamese cat is a pure housecat, but she slipped outside a few days ago and now we can't find her.

Richie snorts, "I can get even with you guys any time I want." He growls, "And you," he points at me, Balona style, with his thumb, "you may yet feel my wrath." Richie sounds just like an evil character out of a TV cartoon. Of course, he *is* evil. He stalks up the steps into his house. I decide to forget that Richie weeps because he has problems. Everybody has problems, and problems like Richie's are no reason to forgive his being a pig and a bully.

I suppose I could try to interview a young person for my *Korndogger* assignment. Richie would be an interesting subject. Everybody knows that he deals dope to kids, is certified as a real criminal with a juvenile crime record, has a variety of criminal enterprises and contacts.

But I suspect that, after Richie's assault this noon on girlfriend Sheba, Constable Cod will soon arrive, and Richie will be hauled off again to Runcible Hall, Chaud County's juvenile jail where, he brags, he has learned more from fellow inmates than he ever learned in Balona classrooms. He spends a good deal of time there. On the other hand, kids know that Richie Kuhl gets away with more than he's ever punished for, despite his self-pity.

Richie doesn't want me to "defend" myself against him. I think he backs away from combat with me because of my aikido study. He probably thinks I might put him down and humiliate him. That's possible, but because I'm no great expert in that martial art, it's unlikely.

A while back he got me to arm-wrestle with him, dared me, probably wanting to boast about his toughness. Physically, I am very strong—a fact I have learned not to brag about—and smacked his arm flat on our backyard picnic table three times in a row. Afterwards he said, "Well, I had a sore shoulder and, besides, I was giving you a break." He's a big endomorph and even older than Jack. He's now possibly stronger than I, so although I have found that a sizzling yellow-green aura typically declares its owner to be a blowhard and a coward, I'm somewhat relieved he gave up today without a fight.

I should know better than to threaten. Daddy always makes a sour face when he hears threatening language from anybody. I'm sure that Mommy tut-tuts and wags her head if she hears it from me. But watching Richie back down is worth the risk.

I get along very well with my classmates, but am really close friends with nobody. It seems that when you're seen as "smart," people are not eager to hang with you. That's all right with me. More or less.

I am friendly and polite, always write thank-you notes when I've received a gift, help my daddy and my grand-parents with household chores. Sometimes I mow the lawn and help in the kitchen where Daddy used to be chief cook. I try especially hard to be charitable to my daddy's wife. I have always made my bed and done the family laundry, ever since my mother passed over.

It's not exactly true that I have no close friends. It's that there are very few people around who share my interests. Jack does, and is somebody I trust. I can tell him anything, and he treats me like a human being. Almost always. He did tell me recently, "You are acting the know-it-all again. Don't be arrogant."

I'm not arrogant. I am simply comfortable with my intelligence.

And Claire is likely going to be a friend, possibly a close friend. She's hugely musical and a whiz with watercolors and oil paints. Although she's blue-eyed and very, very blonde, in some ways she's a lot like me: sort of cool-headed and sensible and logical. I appreciate that.

Most kids don't seem to like my kind of distant attitude in their friends. They seem to want all their friends to be warm and fuzzy and silly, giggling and whispering. That's not the way I am. I tend to follow my mother's advice. "Whatever others may do, go ahead and be yourself," she says.

I have also discovered something about myself. I very much enjoy what is unusual. Getting the *Korndogger* back on a permanent track is not something I could do, and nobody expects it of me, a junior high kid.

But perhaps I can yet find someone to interview who is both interesting and unusual, and maybe my story could help bring the paper up to snuff.

4

Reporter intensifies search for unusual interview subject

As an eager aspiring reporter, I hopalong up to the *Courier* office on Front Street and ask Mr. Preene if I might take a peek at his subscription list. It seems to me that interesting people probably read the newspaper. At least, newspaper readers might be a place to begin my search for interesting old folks to interview.

"We can't let just anybody go through our records, Tery," says publisher Mr. Saint Patrick Preene, another actual relative of my new sister Claire.

I put on a hurt look. "I thought that since I'm now working for the *Korndogger* I might be granted preference."

Mr. Preene has a weight problem and wheezes as he trudges from his office to the front desk where I await his pleasure. "Thought you might be granted preference, eh?

You sound like your grandpa," says Mr. Preene, "and he's older than I am. Oh, well, since your daddy works for me, I might consider your request and grant you some preference." He stops and freezes, dramatically. "Oh. Oh. On the other hand, maybe first I should find out what it is you want to know about our readers. Hmm? After all, you might be a terrorist in disguise." He wheezes a chuckle.

So I tell Mr. Preene about my assignment.

He nods several times. "Good idear. You want to do somebody interesting, you could maybe interview my good old friend Mr. D. H. Carp."

Mr. D. H. Carp is our full-time grocer and part-time former Assemblyperson, appointed a couple of times, but never actually elected. I know that Mr. Preene has served as Mr. Carp's campaign manager. Mr. Carp's always making speeches in which he relates his life story.

"But doesn't everybody already knows everything there is to know about Mr. D. H. Carp?" I suggest this as politely as I am able.

"Well, now. I'm sure there's something Mr. D. H. Carp hasn't leaked out yet." Mr. Preene scratches his scalp and purses his purple lips. "Well, maybe we better let that rest for now. You say you want somebody interesting. Doesn't have to be presently employed, eksedra? Like it could be a retired old person? Maybe an old old person?"

I haven't yet mentioned my original old folks idea, but Mr. Preene homes right in on it, as if he has read my mind.

"Try the Jolly Times. You could get old Kon Chaud to…no. Say, I bet you could maybe get Junior Kuhl to talk. Maybe. Nobody has got him to say anything unexaggerated for the last twenty years, but maybe you got charms to soothe the savage old beast." He makes a mouth as if he's processing a bad taste. "Jolly Times. What a name for that old firetrap. They ought to tear the place down before the environment over there beats old age as the chief cause of death."

I knew of Mr. Junior Kuhl, Balona's oldest living resident at the Jolly Times Rest Home. A popular insult that young guys use to put down another young guy is, "You're lookin' buff as Junior Kuhl." If Junior Kuhl is mentioned at all it is to remark that he is *difficult*. I say, "I hadn't thought of Mr. Junior Kuhl as a subject."

"You could do worse. Junior's not so bad. He's been through some interesting times. If you could get him to talk serious, you'd have yourself a story or two." He moves his lips sideways, a smile. "If you could get Junior to actually talk, maybe even open up some, I might be persuaded to give you a job myself.

"Junior's the son of old Saneyor Julius. y'know, so he's well over a hundred years old. If you get anything at all, it'll probably interest somebody." He makes another mouth, this one as if he's tasted something decidedly bitter. "But probably not your *Korndogger* readers. Teens don't read anything any more. Certainly not my good old newspaper."

"Mr. Preene, I read all the time."

"Well, your daddy says you're a prodigy or something. That's different. That's not your typical teen."

I don't mention that technically I am not yet a teen, but it's nice to know that maybe Daddy bragged about me.

I call administrator Mr. Carbunzle at the Jolly Times Rest Home, a place down First Avenue, an easy bike ride from my home. I identify myself, and ask if it might be possible to interview Mr. Junior Kuhl. The response is at first only breathing and sort of a groan, then, "Well, Mr. Kuhl gets just a few visitors and isn't very communicative in just a polite way. He complains about thieves and criminals stealing from him, so you would have to be prepared for such fantasies." Mr. Carbunzle clears his throat at some length. "I mean, we got a secure place here. Just very secure. Oh." Mr. Carbunzle now sounds alarmed. "You talk like a young lady. You're not a young lady, are you? You are? I don't know if you would just want to be around Mr. Junior Kuhl, since he's just not all that presentable, if you know what I mean."

I say, "I'll be happy to take my chances and, if it doesn't work out, I'll leave as gracefully as I can."

"Would you need a member of my staff to just sit in there with you, sort of just like a chaperone? You wouldn't need that, would you?" It sounds to me as if Zachary's father, lawyer Mr. Kenworth Burnross, might even now be busy suing Jolly Times, and Mr. Carbunzle is feeling the pain.

I ask, "Is Mr. Junior Kuhl very active physically?"

"Mr. Junior Kuhl is as active as one can be at about a 105-plus-years old, which is just not very active. But he does have a loud voice when he just wants to be heard."

I arrange with Mr. Carbunzle to visit Mr. Kuhl this very evening. Quitting our conversation, I hear Mr. Carbunzle sigh. Of course, I have never met Mr. Junior Kuhl, but I doubt that I'll find meeting a really, really old person to be a shock.

I expect Mr. Junior Kuhl to look ancient.

The evening is pleasant, warm. I return to the Jolly Times Rest Home on my bike for the iterview. Late in the afternoon, King Korndog opens the ovens and the redolence of baked korndogs is wafted all over Balona. Although I avoid eating King Korndogs if at all possible, the bakery smell does stimulate one's appetite.

Lawns are greening now. Balona homeowners are proud of their flowerbeds, camellias, rhododendrons, so early summer in Balona is beautiful.

Late summer is something else, what with daytime temperature often reaching into the low hundreds. On very hot days I may not ride my bike, a very old job I bought for ten dollars from Richie Kuhl's big brother Joseph. But today the scale on the "Hannibal Chaud's Funerals" thermometer Daddy screwed onto one of our porch posts reads only eighty degrees. "It's ugly," Daddy admitted about the thermometer, "but it works and it's neighborly." That's a Balona attitude.

My bicycle has a big soft seat, wide balloon tires, and coaster brakes. It originally belonged to Joseph's father, Mr. Kenworth Kuhl, who refers to it as "Hopalong Cassidy," probably a rodeo star from days gone by. Mr. Kuhl didn't want Joseph to sell it to me, until I promised to continue calling it Hopalong.

I restored Hopalong myself, took him completely apart, wiped out the dirt and scraped off the rust. I had his coaster brake in pieces, reassembling the brake only after each component glistened.

I worked over all the metal parts carefully with emery cloth, brushed on two smooth coats of blue enamel, rewired the horn, and installed a fresh battery. Daddy came out, gave me a few mechanical pointers, and watched my progress. "Good job," he said, after beeping the horn.

Most Balona kids who ride bikes nowadays browbeat their parents into buying them fashionable multi-speed racers or mountain bikes.

Kids snicker at Hopalong. But my bike is unique, and his one-of-a-kindness is enjoyable for me. Hiking my leg over his bar is no problem.

On Hopalong, it takes me less than five minutes to get to my destination.

At the Jolly Times Rest Home, flower beds are clustered around the entrance, sort of messy what with weeds interlacing with petals, but blossoms abound in colors. No place to park my bike, so I lean it unlocked against the green-painted ironwork at the side of the steps where the painter has slopped green paint dribs on the concrete.

The entryway to Jolly Times is set some yards back from the street and is attractive from a distance. Close up you see the many greasy smudges on the glass front door. Entering, you are immediately almost overwhelmed by a bad odor. It's not simply as if they never air the place out, but more like you have stepped into a giant deposit of dog doo. I'll have to think about including that fact in my story.

Old folks in wheel chairs sit row on row looking toward a small-screen TV on a table next to the front window. Many of them are not looking at the TV, but seem to be napping. Those looking at the screen probably cannot see it well because of the afternoon sun's glare through the west-oriented window. The TV sound is very low. The walls are hung with moldy-looking draperies. I do not look forward to spending my aged years in such a place.

A slim dark man with a mustache and slicked-down shiny hair pops up before me. He needs a shave. He wears a white medical coat. The black plastic badge at his lapel is imprinted in white letters, *W. Carbunzle, DIRECTOR.* "Are you the visitor for Mr. Junior Kuhl, miss?" he asks, too close to my face. He could use a slurp of mouthwash. He appears worried, so I smile my nicest, showing just-brushed teeth.

I nod like a bobblehead. "I'm Tery Ordway," I say.

"We're almost finished with our afternoon recreation period," he says, "but Mr. Junior Kuhl says he doesn't care for our recreation, so he often just stays in his suite." Mr. Carbunzle points at a hallway off the big room. "Second door on the right." He hesitates, then adds, "I hope you are careful. Leave the door open." Perhaps this will be an assignment-with-danger.

At Mr. Junior Kuhl's door I hear what sounds like a conversation in progress. I knock, but there is no invitation to enter. I push the door open enough to see what might be going on.

I observe a figure in an overstuffed chair by the single window, head nodding onto his chest, his eyes closed. He is speaking not quite distinctly, saying something coversational like, "Well, now. Happy. Sounds pretty good."

I enter and the door closes itself behind me. So much for leaving the door open.

Mumbling to himself, Mr. Junior Kuhl does not appear to offer a major threat, but does present me with my first surprise. He still has all his hair. It's snow white and it curls around his sort of pointed ears and down onto his forehead very much like his namesake, Julius Caesar or an old Vulcan. In the first place I thought it surprising that a 105-year-old man would have all his hair, but that's not the biggest surprise. I expected this really, really old person to be all wrinkled. I was wrong.

Mr. Junior Kuhl's cheeks do not sag. Even obviously without teeth, his face is nicely puffed out with a pink spot on each side, like a little kid just in out of the cold. Mr. Kuhl is wearing a heavy navy-blue robe that is so long it covers his ankles.

He holds the robe's collar closed, as if he is trying to conserve heat on this warm evening.

"Mr. Junior Kuhl?"

Mr. Kuhl looks up, his expression startled. A pointing thumb emerges from the robe-holding fist, indicating the unfolded metal chair across from him.

"Might as well sit down instead of rustling around, sonny. Brung me something chewable this time?"

"It's Tery Ordway, Mr. Kuhl. Mr. Carbunzle said I could visit with you."

"Feels like December. Is it December?"

"No, sir. It's June."

"I was just testing you, boy. C'mon, sit down. There's nothing loose to pick up this time, so just sit down and keep company for a change."

I am wearing a light sweater over a blouse and a skirt. I sit in the folding metal chair opposite his, pull up my stockings, open my notebook. He leans forward and squints at my legs. "Ah, you're not a sonny, after all. It's a female, right?"

"I'm from the Balona High School *Korndogger*, here to interview you about a feature story I'll write about some of your experiences."

"Balona High School. You're never supposed to call it Big Baloney, y'know, or you'll turn into a pillar of salt. You didn't know that? I went to Big Baloney myself, y'know. Back in the days when they taught you. How to be high-class. How to read and write."

"We're learning to read and write just fine nowadays, thank you, Mr. Kuhl."

Perhaps my response is a bit sharp. I bite my tongue.

"You're pretty salty already, young woman. Say right out what you mean. Mind if I ask how old you are?"

"I'll be thirteen." No use saying my exact age, as grown-ups typically see a twelve-year-old as a child. "In the eighth grade in the fall. I'm a good reader and have a few talents."

"I betcha do," he says. "But y'know, when you get old, like me, you've lost so much that all you got is memories. You don't really pay much attention to other people."

I say, "I'll be writing a story about your experiences."

"Lost a lot of those, y'know. Don'tcha have to practically holler for me to hear you? That's why I got you to sit so close here. It bother you? Well, it don't matter much. Poppy always says I don't listen anyways."

He shows his gums. "Of course I haven't lost my good looks, have I? But I don't see all that much really clear, y'know. Kenworth's got to come over and read me my *Courier*."

Unlike the rest of his surprising face, Mr. Kuhl's eyes do appear old. They are faded blue, like a breast feather from a baby jay. "When you get this way, lots of stuff gets by you. That don't matter, since it don't affect you any more. But then you spend a lot of time just thinking some about what it'll be like then."

He pauses, looks blank.

I prompt, "...'then'?"

"Ah, you're listening. Rare thing, that anybody will listen to an old man." He blows his nose on his sleeve, looks at me as he wipes his palm over the shiny spot, shrugs. "*Then* is when I'm gone. G-o-n. Most old folks think about what's over there on the other side, y'know. Young people don't think about that. Young people are gonna live forever. I thought that way."

He points his thumb at me. "You think that way? No? But it wasn't the looting and the killing. Or the threats or the thirst and hunger that was the bad part. Or carrying heavy stuff for miles and miles, until the wheelbarrow. I

41

don't think all that much about those things. No, it was the fire. Think about that all my life."

I intrude when I should listen.

"What fire is that?" I ask. "Oh, the Balona fires last year, when the Oliver burned, and then the OK Hotel and then Purity Palace. Yes, mysterious fires. Terrible."

"No, no. Not them. I'm talking the fire where the little ones was. Where the biggest flames was. When the building fell down. But right now I got to take lunch."

I don't need to look at my wristwatch. By my internal time-sense, it is almost 7:00 P.M.

"I take lunch when I feel hungry, y'know. Right now I feel hungry. No offense meant."

He rustles behind him in his chair and his robe falls open, revealing a heart-shaped silver locket suspended on a silver chain. Both the locket and chain appear to need a good polishing.

He drags out a crushed brown paper bag from under one of several stained tan-corduroy pillows. "Grandson Kenworth brings me a sangwidge to snack on. Since they don't feed you in this place."

Mr. Kuhl stops his movements and looks at the ceiling.

"Kenworth's not been to see me lately. I think it was the fat boy brought me this here sangwidge. Now, I ask you, who was that fat boy, I wonder?" Mr. Kuhl speaks in gasps and bursts, incomplete sentences, but his voice has become stronger as he speaks, and the sound of it is clear. I think Claire who is so musical would say the tone is sweet, and that quality is as surprising as is the smoothness of his skin and the fullness of his head of hair.

The eyes are red-rimmed, as if he might have spent the day weeping, but that redness might be attributed to the strain of his age.

Now from the hallway come shrieks, groans, a muffled curse, clatter, squeaky sounds like wheels in need of oil. The evening recreation is breaking up and residents are being returned to their rooms, "suites," as Mr. Carbunzle has referred to them.

"Y'know," he says, "a man could fade away at this place. Old Kon Chaud down the hall? Can't even talk any more. From his starvation. Not to speak of his constipation. And he's younger'n me."

Mr. Kuhl leans toward me, confidentially. "I don't have the constipation, y'know. But you got to have your emergency bag. For emergencies. You carry an emergency bag? No?"

He pauses for a moment. "I should've tried to get in there. Save those babies. But I guess nobody could. Couldn't get to 'em. So it wasn't exactly my fault. Poppy tried. Couldn't stop crying. Mama, too. I think about 'em. Can still hear 'em. You think there won't be no emergency. But let me tell you, there'll always be some kind of a big emergency. And you better be ready for it."

"Well, I guess you're ready for it, Mr. Kuhl."

"Dang tootin' I'm ready. Like we used to say in the old days, I'm ready for Hezzie."

5

Diligent preparation enhances interview process

Mr. Junior Kuhl tugs at his crushed paper bag, his emergency bag. "I got a couple other emergency bags hid away, lem'me tell you. One's got a water bottle in it, for thirst. Lucky I got one grandson thinks about me. My own boys never cared for me. But my Grandson Kenworth does. Crazy as a loon. But he thinks about me. Once and a while brings me a sangwidge. See?"

The sandwich peeps out of the bag in what looks like a paper-towel wrapping. The sandwich is considerably flattened and leaking what surely must be peanut butter from various of its dimensions.

"I told Kenworth I don't much like the crunchy kind. Hard on the gums, y'know. Maybe it was the fat boy brung this sangwidge here, not Kenworth." Mr. Kuhl chews, scowls. "Ouch. Crunchy."

Mr. Kuhl uses a finger to adjust the contents of his cheek. "Did I say hard on the gums? Well, root hog or die. I wonder who that boy is."

Mr. Kuhl appears to have no teeth, but he has tucked into his sandwich rapidly, with lots of wheezing, smacking, and lip-wiping-with-sleeve.

"Pardon the mess here," he says. "This place got no refinement, y'know. No napkins ever. And they steal from you. Steal your stuff, you don't sleep on it. Come in here in the night. Rustle around in your stuff. If I was the governor, I'd terminate 'em, wipe 'em out."

Sitting close, I have immediately discovered that Mr. Kuhl does not smell nearly as bad as the larger Jolly Times environment. He actually has sweet breath. The breath is moist, too, probably resulting from his lack of teeth, and he lisps and sprays when speaking. So I try to lean away a bit.

But Mr. Kuhl is also a toucher and keeps leaning forward to touch my arm or my hand to emphasize points in his conversation. He doesn't touch my knees, and he doesn't squeeze; only touches with his fingertips. And he looks directly into my eyes when he touches, probably trying to cement a connection.

While Mr. Kuhl is occupied with his postprandial cleanup I am reminded of Daddy. Daddy, who smells good all year, smells usually like Old Spice, since that's what I give him every Christmas. He would use it even if he didn't like it, because he's a really good man. Probably he does still love me some, for why else would he donate to the *Korndogger*? I should ask him does he actually like Old Spice.

Probably he doesn't like my Old Spice gift as much as the French-sounding after-shave lotion Penny gave him.

On the other hand, when I sniff around him a bit, it seems that probably he doesn't use hers much yet.

Most Balona women simply smell loud. I don't know how to explain it in other terms. But Penny rarely uses perfume, smells generally clean and sort of lemony, which is nice to be around. My daddy seems to think so, too.

When my Original Mommy was active on this plane, she liked "Charlie," an inexpensive scent I still like. She has suggested that she would like to enjoy the smell of Old Spice again if she were able to.

It takes Mr. Junior Kuhl no time at all to consume his sandwich, but he requires a much longer time to finish his chewings, gum-cleanings, and lip-wipings. Finally, Mr. Kuhl makes a slight burp, excuses himself, and addresses me.

"What's your name again?" He seems to have forgotten why I am visiting. I tell him once again, spelling the name, repeating it when he leans forward, turning his head the better to hear.

I decide not to explain the single-r spelling, that Tery is American for Teru, a Japanese name meaning sunshine, in honor of Obahchan, my Japanese grandma.

Mr. Kuhl hacks and coughs, clearing his peanut-buttered throat for several seconds. "I knew a lady name of Theresa. No more, of course. Called her Terry, too. But she didn't like to be called that. 'Not respectful, you calling me that. You should call me Theresa,' she kept saying. I called her Terry anyways."

He squints his eyes, stares at the floor. "You know Theresa?" He shakes his head. "No, I guess not. Gone w-e-s-t, a long time ago."

"I'm sorry." I say this most sincerely, as his face is suddenly so sad. and I am touched by that.

"No need. Happens to us all. Gonna happen to me soon enough, Poppy tells me." He sighs. "Wisht I was seventy-five again. Really good year for both of us." He pulls the locket and its chain up and over his head, holds it in his fist, massaging the tarnished metal with his thumb. He turns his head away and gazes out the window. Any view is obscured by a dense euonymous growing next to the window, the bush more than head-high, but Mr. Kuhl leans sideways, trying to peer through the shrubbery.

Although with the ready capacity of my memory it's not necessary for me to write anything, I do take a few notes, especially observing that Mr. Junior Kuhl's seventy-fifth year was a really good year.

He turns back, wipes his eyes with forefinger and thumb, and recognizes me again. "I like the way you do that."

"Pardon?" I say.

"I like that you don't fidget. You sit there with your hands on your notebook. And you don't move except your writing fingers once and a while. Most people I know fidget. Have to keep moving. Jiggling their knee or their ankle. Scratching theirselfs. Leaning this way and that. You sit still. That's so nice and peaceful. If it was a hundred years ago I think I would ask you to marry me."

This is a nice surprise. But, given our present ages and circumstances, not all that attractive. I decide to move the dialog forward.

"Mr. Kuhl, you could tell me some stories about Balona in the old days. I bet kids would be interested in your stories."

"Dearie, no kid I ever knew was interested in old days. Except Robin Hood stories. And about wars and pirates. Murders. Stuff like that." He smiles, looks at my shins. "You're wearing long red stockings."

I explain, "I like kneesocks. These are a little warm for June, but I knitted 'em myself. I think they're pretty."

Mr. Kuhl wags his head. "Daisy wore long stockings. Always black. Never red. Said red wasn't stylish."

I decide to ignore argument. "A minute or so ago you said that 'Poppy' told you something. Is Poppy the name of somebody, maybe an employee here?"

"I said *what?* No, I wouldn't say that. You just heard wrong. I'm not crazy." He mutters, "Knock on wood."

"Well, then, you mentioned a fire you think about all the time. Could you talk about that?"

"That was a long, long time ago. Did I say I thought about it all the time? All the time?" He leans forward again and gives me an intense look. "You really interested, are you? Really?"

"Really. Yes." I poise my pencil. It's unnecessary to notify the recorder inside my head.

"Well, maybe I got time to tell you a few things. My old father went over at a hundred-thirteen, so I figger I actually got a little time yet."

"...went over?"

"He passed over, kiddo. I hate to mention the word, so I'll spell it for you: d-i-d-e. How old are you again? Twenty, you said?"

"Uh, twelve."

"All right, I'll tell you about when I was near that age. Twelve is pretty dumb, as you may remember. But at the time I thought I knew everything." Mr. Kuhl settles back in his chair.

The locket still in his hand, he adjusts his robe, clears his throat. "Well, sir, my family had went from Gold Hill over to Nevada where Poppy tried to homestead in the desert. Went broke. Then went to Grass Valley where Poppy tried to mine for gold in the old holes. Went broke." Mr. Kuhl wags his head.

"Then went down to Sacramento where Poppy tried to teach himself to be a professional gambler. Went broke again, and we had to get out of town quick.

"All that time I was either not there at all or else I was a little kid. After a while I grew up some and knew more.

"So we moved over to San Francisco where Poppy worked on the docks. Got so he couldn't hold anything in his hands they was so cramped up from grabbing and lifting heavy stuff." Mr. Kuhl dramatizes a bit, making claws of his fingers by way of illustration. "We lived in a flat up above a drugstore at William and McAllister Streets. School up four blocks and fire station down one. You know the place? No? Well, William was a short little street. Gone now anyways, y'know. Wiped out, like the buildings and the people. I'll tell you shortly how come they're gone. Anyways, about Poppy's hands. Poppy used to come home from the docks, and we'd take turns massaging his hands. With lard mixed with wintergreen.

"You know an amazing thing about your memory? Well, I'll tell you. When you get old you can't remember where you put your pencil or your teeth. Or your sangwidge. But you can remember the color of your first toy. Figger that, won't you." Mr. Kuhl wags his head again, wonderingly. "William and McAllister Streets.

"Then a little while later, when we had that most terrible, awful time, Poppy heard about how you could make a potfull of money growing asparagrass and potatoes and sugarbeets over here in the delta. So since we was all practically starving, me especially, and was living under the sky, Poppy used almost but not quite the last dollars of his hero-reward money to buy us a buckboard. Moved

50

all of us, my mama, brothers and sister, them as was left, came on over here to Balona. But that was after our place had burnt down and — did I already say it? — we was out in the street. Everything gone. Again."

I lean toward him, encouraging the speaker, I hope. "Your house burned. That sounds terribly exciting."

"That was the hot and smelly and sad and scary part. Of course, I wasn't too scared." He frowns. "Well, yes, I was. It was scary and terrible both, yes. But the exciting part was just before the fire. And the best part, the good part I like to remember, was before that, with the horses."

I intrude again. "I love horses."

Mr. Kuhl sighs, ignoring my comment. "I figger I'll take me a nap for a spell. You can wait right there, though. Won't take long."

We sit there "for a spell," he nodding onto his chest, and I formulating questions. I want to be sure to ask him about something he has already said: His father's hero-reward money. That sounds interesting.

And the *Poppy* he seemed to be having a conversation with as I entered his room. Who is Poppy? It's an unusual nickname for a friend. Possibly a girlfriend? Probably his father.

It's unlikely that Mr. Junior Kuhl has the same relationship to his dead father that I have with my dead mother. But it would be interesting to discover if "Poppy" is his father and Mr. Junior Kuhl actually has conversations the way I am able to speak with Mommy. If this is the case, it will be the first time I have found another person granted the same blessing.

Of course, if true, I can't write about it for the record, for readers would brand my report as fabrication. I had a bad habit that I am training out of myself. Even when I was beginning the interview with Mr. Junior Kuhl, I tried to guess what he was going to say, and so I'd ask a question to sort of surprise him. I did get some interesting reactions that way. But when you do that, you interrupt your interviewee's train of thought.

My daddy is not a reporter, but he says he's often heard many amateur reporters interrupting their subjects. It's better if you listen, he says. Just listen and act like you appreciate what you hear.

I have noticed that Daddy never interrupts Penny.

I cough several times, until Mr. Kuhl rouses himself. "Tell about the horses," I prod, instead of listening.

"I'll get to 'em, if you'll just hold yours." Mr. Kuhl wheezes a chuckle, quite awake again.

A good-looking T-shirted young Asian man opens the door, pokes his head, shoulder, and one huge bicep into the room. "Everything all right, Mr. Kuhl?"

"All right, Kevin. You can go away. I'm safe with this one." Both men chuckle, and Kevin closes the door.

"Kevin is a pain, chews me out for singing my songs. But except for that, Kevin is a good boy. Kevin is a Japanese fellow, y'know. You can tell by looking. Only Japanese people I know of in Balona besides Kevin is young Alex Ordway's wife. He brought her from over there. Across the water. Pretty little lady plays the piano without looking at the notes. Japanese people live in Lodi and Delta City, though. Plenty of 'em nowadays. Not many in the old days, though. Mostly Chinese and Mexicans then. They called my daddy Saneyor. Called me Saneyor Ho-ven."

Mr. Kuhl seems to examine the wall, lost in thought.

While Mr. Kuhl thinks about foreigners in general, I notice that the walls of his room are not clean. They are papered with a flower-printed material that seems to hang loose in places, as if a vertical gopher is making trips of discovery about the room. The paper seems ready to drop from the wall, a real eyesore. I observe to myself that it will be a whole lot safer if Mr. Kuhl never uses matches or lights candles in this place. Then, as the conversation has been about Mr. Kuhl's father, I consider my own, and how he follows Penny around.

I move our conference along by prompting Mr. Kuhl again. "Your father was good."

"Well, I already said that. He hardly ever whupped me. Then only because I deserved it." Mr. Kuhl's eyes become wet-looking, and he gazes into his lap, snuffling, soon becomes quiet again.

I think about trying to change the subject. Recently, I have come to realize that when somebody is talking and tears come into his eyes, it's another reason to shut up and listen. But in this interview I am eager for more facts. I like facts, not sentiments especially.

For example, it's a fact, strange but true, that Mr. Kuhl's grandson, Mr. Kenworth Kuhl, has an affirmative aura. He gives off a beautiful, pale yellow, gentle signal that includes some puzzling black dots. His grandfather, this Mr. Junior Kuhl, has a pink aura that still faintly sparkles lavender, the sparkling not a sure indicator of the charitable person he appears to be.

Mr. Kuhl turns his head and squints at me straight on, frowning, as if seeing me for the first time.

"Y'know, even with your red socks, you are a really handsome young woman. I like black eyes. The way you keep your head up. You probably got foreign blood, though, or Indian, gives you those eyes."

I don't get that kind of compliment very often, you might say. But then he continues: "But I like better long-haired-women, y'know. I like black hair like you got, all right, but longer than yours. Oh, well, modren times. Red stockings." He sighs. "Well, I guess I better say about some things that happened back then."

I settle back now lubricated with compliments, and begin a new page in my notebook.

6

Pioneer recounts hair-raising incidents

MR. JUNIOR KUHL: There in San Francisco, Mama cleaned and scrubbed. Poppy mostly slept. We'd all have to be real quiet and pass by his door on our tippy-toes. But sometimes Poppy would spend hours playing cards with himself at our dinner table.

"Conserving my energy," he would say, "and practicing my craft." Since when he got fired from his job on the docks, he had to go out and try to make a living at cards by night. Mama always said that Poppy was not a lucky man. Except that he found her.

Then Poppy would whisper behind his hand, "It was her that found me."

TERY: This is all about when your family lived in San Francisco.

MR. KUHL: That's what I been talking about, girl.

TERY: Sorry. I should pay closer attention.

MR. KUHL: Well, that's all right. The fat boy who brung me my sangwidge never pays attention. He keeps poking around the room, looking at my stuff, touching it. I tell him to sit down and chew the fat for a while. But then he takes off. I wonder who that fat boy is.

TERY: You said your father was unlucky?

MR. KUHL: I never did believe Poppy telling about himself being unlucky. Just the opposite in fact. When we got over here to Balona, him and me both made a mint. Anyways, back to The City back in the old days.

I got me a great job mucking out the stables on the corner, just a block down from us on McAllister. At the fire house that was there at the time. Grover was blue-jealous. The job didn't pay me much, nothing at all at first, only the pleasure a kid can get, just hanging out around an exciting place.

But after a while, when I got to doing good work, they give me some every week. I give it up to my ma, most of it, saved some for candy and tobacco.

TERY: You were how old?

MR. KUHL: Well, now, I figger I was about eleven or twelve. Oh, you caught that about the tobacco. Yeah, in those days, kids would try to ape their elders, and I was a kid. Not like nowadays when kids will go hog wild, trying to ape theirselfs.

But Captain Sullivan wouldn't let anybody smoke around the place, y'know. Just like Wendel and Kevin won't let the old folks smoke around here. Account of the fire problem, Kevin says.

We get a fire drill every month. But nobody ever pays attention to it. Somebody clangs a big bell. Everybody just goes back to sleep. Nobody cares.

Anyways, I never did smoke. Dirty habit. Back in the old days none of our firemen smoked. At least, on duty. They chewed tobacco. Then they spat their tobacco juice all over the pucky-pile. Some of 'em, to be high-class and sanitary, kept a cup to spit into if they was far off from a pile. Carried their spit-cups around with 'em. After they got a full cup, poured their spit onto the pucky-pile. Sometimes there was some confusion about a cup. Whether it was your spit-cup or your coffee cup? Lots of sport there, y'know.

Anyways, I had to have something to chew, too, like any other fireman. Naturally, I couldn't help but swallow some tobacco juice, and it right away made me sick. So, to be manly about it, I bought me some likrish. It'll work up spit for you like a champion, y'know. Firemen didn't know the difference.

Tasted a whole lot better. Made your tongue and teeth and spit glorious black. And since you could swallow your nice sweet spit, you didn't have to carry that spit-cup around with you.

TERY: [Feeling just a bit queasy, I need to try to change the subject.] What were your duties, Mr. Kuhl?

MR. KUHL: Well, what you do when you muck out stables is they give you a pitchfork and...you probably don't know what a pitchfork is. Well, it's a tool, of course. A fork you pitch with! Not exactly like a shovel. Got some sharp steel tines you can stick into hay and pick it up.

Once you learn how. You go into the horse stalls mostly when the horses are out working or at a fire. And you pick up the horse-pucky and pee-wet hay on your pitchfork. And you throw it on a big pile. Later, you move the pile onto a wagon that gets hauled out and dumped in the bay where they threw all the trash of the city.

Nowadays if you took your pencil there and flung it the bay they'd haul you off to jail, they're so very particular. But in the old days when I was a kid, that's what you did with all the city's trash. Threw it in the bay.

Nowadays they got huge big houses and stores built over on top of that trash. But trash is not bedrock, y'know.

Poppy says that someday those houses and stores are gonna quiver theirselfs straight downwards into salt water, since a huge big quake is sure to happen there again.

TERY: [Mr. Kuhl drifts off for a while. I wait a minute.] You mentioned that Poppy tells you...

MR. KUHL: T-t-t-ells? Tells me? No, I never did. I never said Poppy tells me *nothing*. I'm not off of my rocker. I was talking about trash.

TERY: And you threw the horse-pucky on a big pile.

MR. KUHL: You maybe need to listen closer, since that's something I already did say. Anyways, sometimes you had to muck-out while a horse was in his stall. You had to be real careful. Those horses had huge big feet and sharp teeth. Would once and a while nip at you with those choppers and chewers.

Sam was my boss. He was in charge of the horses in my station. Once and a while when I first started, he would send me into the stall with a hardscrabble horse. One that was not in a good mood.

"Just to make sure the kid is careful," Sam would say to the other firemen. Everybody would laugh. But they would all watch to see if I got stepped on or nipped at. Both of which did happen. After a while, I got to be an old hand. When a new kid came around for a job, I would get to assign him to a stall. He would get stepped on and nipped. Just for fun, mind you. Back in those days, people wasn't as mean as they are today. But still they liked their fun rough. And they wouldn't sue you just for a simple broken toe.

Mostly the horses was nice. Appreciated you giving them a carrot. Or a piece of apple. You ever smelt a horse close up? Yeah? Well, then you know that horses got a special horse-smell. There's your general horse smell. And then there's your individual horse's smell.

It's just like people.

You go to into the movie-show nowadays, and besides the popcorn, I betcha it smells like general sweat in there. Used to anyways at the Oliver. But over in somebody's yard, you get up next to a guy cutting wood with an axe. You can smell the wood. But there's his own smell hanging in the air, too. Everybody's different. Everything's got his own little personality. At least, that's what I figured out whilst I was wiping down and washing up and currying those horses.

[Mr. Kuhl nods to himself.]

After a while, I had showed Sam and the others I wasn't afraid of a few horsenips and bumps. So Captain Sullivan let me help with the grooming.

When the horses wasn't busy elsewhere.

Oh yes, in those days horses was really busy. It wasn't your Mack truck nor your Peterbilt nor your Kenworth did the hard work. It was horses pulled near everything.

TERY: [Interrupting.] Did you have streetcars then?

MR. KUHL: Well, sir, we did have streetcars at that time. Yes, indeedy, electric ones. On the flatland. And we had the cable cars for the steep hills.

And some people already had automobiles. If they was rich. Usually big, loud, smelly automobiles. Running on gasoline or steam or even electricity. Those things would take over any road. Scare everybody in sight. "Git a horse," us kids would shout. Back in those good old days, whatever the other vehicles, we still had horses. And mules and your occasional jackass everywhere.

When you got horses everywhere, you got, pardon the expression, horse-pucky and horse-pee everywhere. And the smell that goes with it.

Well, sir, you get used to that smell. After a while you never notice stuff like that at all. Just like noticing things nowadays. You hardly notice the diesel smell from the big rigs. Or hear the *thump-thump-thump* vibrations from the teen cars rocking this place at night. I never noticed the horse-pucky smell in the first place.

So it was horses that pulled the wagons that hauled off them tons of horse-pucky that got scraped up from the streets. Horses pulled a few of the streetcars. Our horses pulled regular trash wagons, y'know. A big city like San Francisco's got a lot of trash to haul off every day.

Horses pulled the tank wagons that filled the fire cisterns and watered-down the streets whenever they got too dusty. Horses pulled the milk wagons. And the vegetable wagons. And the tinkers and gypsy wagons. And taxis.

Our fire department had hundreds of big, strong horses. Of course, at our station, we had only eight at a time. But there was stations all over the city. If there was a fire, those horses pulled their engines, slipping and sliding and straining up those hills. Like race champions.

But if there was no fire, you couldn't have all those horses just lounging about in their stalls eating bon-bons like fine ladies, doing nothing. They had to work. And so they did other hauling chores, like pull the trash wagons and the ash wagons. And the pucky wagons, of course.

Then, when there was a fire, everyone could hear the fire bells ringing. And the garbage men and the ash men and the water men unhitched our horses. And those great beasts ran straight back to their fire houses. Just like your homing pigeons.

[Mr. Kuhl flaps his arms by way of illustration.]

And then those fine horses backed theirselfs into their shafts, smooth as a whistle. Right back to their places at the pumper. You ever heard of such a thing?

TERY: I never heard of such a thing.

MR. KUHL: Well, that's a fact. You just ask anybody that was there at the time. [He winks at me.]

TERY: A pumper, you said.

MR. KUHL: Well, now, you got to understand something about those days. There wasn't many automobile trucks. Oh, you'd see those things around. Kind of like freaks, drove around by high-falutin merchants or rich farmers. And you couldn't never drive an automobile all the way up that California Street grade the way the cable cars can.

We had cable cars running up and down lots of those hills in the old days. The usual auto there, bit off more than he could chew, would just poop out on you.

But your great old horse could even pull engines up some of those hills. If the hill wasn't too steep and slick and the load too heavy. So it took good old horses—teams of 'em—to pull the engines.

To make the pumps work they didn't yet use motor engines run by gasoline or diesel. You used steam engines up there on top of the engine bed. Coal-fired or oil-fired steam engines powered just about everything in those days. Matter of fact, it wasn't until I was an old man that you no longer had steam engines tugging railroad trains. You never saw a steam engine working? Like a steam locomotive on the rails? A pity you missed that beautiful sight.

And the sound of the whistle off of a steam locomotive barreling through the night?

[Mr. Kuhl puts his hand to his ear, as if trying to capture the whistling.] A sad, lonesome, faraway sound. Still gives me a fine chill to recollect it.

But the fire engine pumpers, spurted their water from the strength of that steam engine pump. The firemen would stick a hose down into a fire cistern. That was a huge big tank down in a hole in the street that they kept filled with water for fire service. And the pump would suck that water right up. Send it out through another hose so snaky powerful that sometimes two men had to hold on to it. And the firemen would aim that hose. Put out the fire with that huge big squirt. That was steam power. Well, it'll come back in your lifetime, mark my words, girl.

So, anyways, they put out most fires. Some fires got too big to put out. The firemen had to run away. But that was later. And them good old sweaty horses, them dear beasts, hot and heavy as it would get, stayed right where they was supposed to, sparks flying and all.

TERY: [Mr. Kuhl chokes up at this point and has to wipe his eyes and blow his nose on a tissue I hand him.]

MR. KUHL: Then, when they got back to the firehouse after a fire where the horses had worked hard, talk about a horsey smell. Well, we rubbed those boys down. Put their blankets over their tops. Washed their mouths and noses and under their tails. Let them drink just a little water to cool their mouth. You can't give a hot horse cold water. He'll get sick on you, y'know. So we had to be careful about that. You give a horse some water to drink when he wakes up first thing in the morning. Then, after a while, you give him some oats. Then you can rub the boy down.

TERY: All the horses were boys?

MR. KUHL: Makes sense. You don't have a female fireman, do you? Trying to hold them hoses takes a strong man or two. So you probably need strong male horses to do all that pulling and racing.

TERY: Nowadays there are female firefighters in the Delta City Fire Department.

MR. KUHL: Well, that's politics, y'know. Like putting women in the army. Where they can primp and gossip and cause trouble.

TERY: You've been in the military.

MR. KUHL: I was already trading grain and sugar-beets when we got into the first big one. Made my first big bundle. That's how come my boys all got rich in the next one. You can make a lot of money in wartime. But not if you're over there in it, getting shot at and blown up.

TERY: That was the First World War.

MR. KUHL: That's what I just said. We had some boys from Balona go over there. Rush Runcible was in the Pigeon Corps, I think they called it. Where pigeons took messages and flew 'em around up above the gunfire. Rush always liked pigeons. I don't much like pigeon, myself—a dirty bird—but I don't mind a nice dish of squab.

I wonder who that fat boy was. I'm getting awful tired. Whyn't you go home now. You could come back later and bring me a sangwidge.

∾

Mr. Junior Kuhl goes to sleep almost as he finishes speaking, his mouth dropping open and snapping shut as his chin reaches his chest, his locket still clutched in his fist. I leave at once.

So I have completed my first-phase interview with Mr. Junior Kuhl, and he has begun to "open up," as we news hounds say. Of course, he also has begun to fall asleep during our interviews, mumbling so that it is difficult to understand what he is saying. Something about mucking-out pigeon cotes, I think. Mucking-out is not a pleasant expression. But then, it's probably not a pleasant job.

My brother's friend Sal Shaw, my tutor Senta's son, is already in college, has some beautiful horses he lets us ride, and has mentioned mucking-out a few times. I thought it was slang, like bugging out, an expression my grandfather uses and says it's from his wartime experiences. I have figured out that the phrase means *running away scared.* But now I know better about Mr. Kuhl's phrase. I am not quite obsessed with horses.

I am glad Mr. Kuhl loves them, too.

As I leave the Jolly Times Rest Home, Director Carbunzle appears to bow from a distance. He also rubs his hands and moves toward me, but I wave and leave.

The big so-called recreation room through which one enters and leaves is almost empty, except for a bent old man with a sunken chest and a weary appearance leaning over a mop handle, pushing his tool, appearing not to be aware of what he is sweeping. The odor remains, now heavier and mixed with a smell like that of vegetable soup.

All during the last school year my brother Jack volunteered here several hours a week, reading books and newspapers to residents. And playing the piano he described as "a half-step flat from top to bottom." He never discussed this community service.

I'll have to ask him about his view of the place, compare notes.

My good old bicycle with his almost new tires and tubes is waiting for me exactly where I had left him, but now with both tires flat and his front wheel spokes bashed out of kilter.

My foot stamps involuntarily and relieves some of the tension I feel. I have to cough more than a few times. And then I pull up my stockings and center myself in the manner that Master Tri teaches us. I walk Hopalong home, his front wheel now wobbling, scraping his fender with every revolution.

Probably it's someone's wrath that I'm feeling.

7

Reporter almost suffers near-death experience

I now have a lot of items about Mr. Junior Kuhl in my notes, but last night on the phone when I tried to describe them in some detail to Sheba, she constantly interrupted me, saying she wasn't hearing anything *juicy*.

"You got to have some juicy stuff," she complained. "Like did he have some extra-marital sex experiences in the old days, like on the TV. That sort of thing."

I wondered aloud how Mr. Peralta and Mr. Croon and the school community in general would respond to my presenting 105-year-old Mr. Junior Kuhl to Balona High Summer School *Korndogger* readers as a Sex God.

Sheba said, "You like wouldn't have to tell in your story how old he actually is. Right away, that is. You could let my readers — our readers, I guess—stew some in the hot juices of spectation."

"I see," I said. I didn't agree, but withheld my objections, hoping to be able to offer a good counter-argument later.

"I mean," said Sheba, "you said he wasn't all wrinkled up. So he was a studly dude in the old days? Maybe?"

"He talked about a big fire."

"No, no, no. We got fires in Balona all the time." Sheba *tsked,* sounded disgusted. "Nothing juicy about fires." She sniffed.

"He mentioned that his father was called a hero."

"Well, that might work." She suddenly sounded encouraged. "You got to like squeeze more out of him, y'know."

"Yes. I'll go back."

"You do that. Better do that pretty soon, since we got deadlines, y'know." I could hear her blowing her nose. "Actually, you don't have something good pretty soon, I'll take you off of the case." That ended the conversation. My foot tapped spontaneously and I coughed a couple of times. Sheba sounded like the top cop in a detective drama.

~

I close my bedroom door and the blinds, sit on my bed, shut my eyes and compose myself, trying to get some advice from my mother. Jack refers to her as Mom, but as I was only five years old when she passed over, I still think of her as Mommy, not Mom or Mother or Ma. Jack says it was 3:30 in the morning when we were awakened by Daddy's sobbing.

I feel now that she is making an appearance but, "Follow your instincts. You'll get it right," is all I can get from her. She seems distant, as if she is in deep thought about something else. She usually expresses herself much more gracefully, helping me figure out knotty problems. I want to ask her opinion about Mr. Junior Kuhl and his interior dialogs. She isn't responding. Maybe she is trying to get me to forget my feelings and consult more with Penny. I go downstairs and do just that.

I am taller than Penny, but she has long copper-red hair, wound up today in sort of a chignon tied with an orange scarf. She has dark brown eyes and clear skin. I am said to be "pretty," but she is unquestionably beautiful, something Daddy has been aware of all along, I'm sure.

Penny likes the color orange and wears it often. She has a gentle light-green aura with no prickles at all. She is still young despite being mother to a seventeen-year-old, for Claire was born when Penny was only fourteen. It's a long, sad short-story that I don't need to recite here. She is a sweet-smelling gentle person who had never married.

Everybody says she will turn out to be a fine wife for Daddy who seems to love her a lot. He hugs her quite often. And I am almost totally happy with her, except that she's always trying to kiss him and touch his arm, his face, his hand. She could be less demonstrative with him.

Penny is mixing something. "Hi, kid. Would you like to lick the bowl?" Her cheeks redden. "I'm sorry, honey. I keep thinking of how Claire has always liked to do that."

"Well," I say, "being as how I am still a kid, I'll lick the bowl for you." And while quizzing her, I sit at the table and lick the bowl, using mostly my finger instead of my tongue. Penny is making a dessert. She likes popcorn and chocolate, both things my daddy likes, too. This dessert is chocolaty.

"You're enjoying being up with the high school kids?"

"They're okay. Different species from my regular friends. Enjoyable enough. Mr. Peralta is nice, too. Sheba Weiner is interesting."

Penny looks at me and smiles. "I do believe you find everyone and everything interesting. That's another of your many talents."

"I'm interviewing Mr. Junior Kuhl for a story I'm supposed to do for the *Korndogger*. But I don't know how to handle it. I mean, I don't have a handle on it. Yet."

"Ah. You said *yet*. I'll bet you figure something out. Before Claire inherited her fortune, I worked for Mr. Junior Kuhl's grandson, Mr. Kenworth Kuhl. I was his secretary."

Penny pauses and appears to be reminiscing. "Mr. Kenworth Kuhl used to visit his grandpa regularly, sometimes every afternoon. I thought that was sweet. Lots of old folks are avoided, even abandoned by their offspring. But Mr. Kenworth Kuhl isn't mean like that. I'll bet Mr. Junior Kuhl will have fascinating things to say."

"Fascinating isn't enough, according to my editor."

"Sheba Weiner is on the staff over there?"

"She's the *Korndogger* editor. You know Sheba?"

"I know her mama." Penny sighs. "I've seen that you have a very good head on your shoulders, and I believe that what you decide will be interesting to everybody."

She leans over, takes my clean-licked bowl, and kisses me on the forehead. Mommy used to kiss me like that. Mommy loved me a lot. The forehead-kiss produces a warm feeling. I think that maybe Penny might actually come to love me. I'm sure my daddy loves her more than he loves me. Even so, I feel like giving Penny a hug, but decide to save it for something more important. I also feel sort of let down, what with no advice forthcoming. I am back to square one: me, myself, and I.

After lunch I pump up Hopalong's tires and use my spoke wrench to repair the damage to his front wheel.

Then I prepare a fine sandwich for Mr. Junior Kuhl. This one not only peanut butter, but also with thinly-sliced ripe banana on white bread. I pare off the crusts to donate to our backyard bird visitors — perhaps including Mr. Kenworth Kuhl's famous magpie — cut the sandwich in several pieces, wrap them up in wax paper, and take off on Hopalong for the Jolly Times Rest Home.

In the distance coming in my direction up First Avenue, is Richie Kuhl. "To save gas," Joseph tells me, Richie often leaves his own motorcycle at home and hitches rides on the back of a friend's motorcycle. He is alleged to have snatched women's purses from that vantage. He is said to brag — I cite Jack here — that one of Richie's favorite tricks is to borrow somebody else's motorcycle, and "key" cars and trucks on the Interstate, ride close to them and dig into their paint as he passes. Richie uses a large iron nail, says Joseph.

I should think that this is a terribly dangerous pastime, but apparently Richie does it all the time. Never been caught.

Richie is now again on a motorcycle, probably his newly acquired machine. As usual, he is not wearing a helmet.

I tighten my grasp on Hopalong's handgrips and begin to recite the mantra that steadies me, lowers my center, and prevents levitation.

I expect Richie to swing by me close enough for me to smell him, but that's not quite what happens. He actually zigs toward me as he passes. As he leans himself and his machine at me, his extended knee and elbow both strike me.

The blow knocks Hopalong and me flying.

As a practitioner of aikido, I have learned how to fall, and I am not even scratched much. That's more than I can say for Hopalong, whose paint will need some touching up. I remain sitting in the gutter next to Pastor Nim Chaud's Tabernacle sidewalk. Richie has stopped some distance down the street. He's wearing his one-sided smirk, probably hoping to see blood. Now he turns his machine around and cruises back towards me. He is going to gloat and brag about how cool he is. "I'm cool, like my name," he is fond of saying at every opportunity.

As Richie approaches in the middle of the street, he manages a wheelie, a maneuver modeled frequently on TV, in which the rider revs his motor so that he can pull the front wheel up, riding about on the rear wheel.

In the midst of Richie's wheelie, we are both surprised. I am rocked back against the curb and Richie sways, he and his cycle both hitting the pavement as if thrown by an invisible giant, the cycle skittering over the gutter and onto the sidewalk, Richie just lying at the edge of the street, part of him on he sidewalk, his back bent over the curb.

I ask myself, Is Richie dead?

"Whoa," says Pastor Nimitz MacArthur Chaud, who has come out of his church, perhaps to check on my wounds. "Earthquake."

"We're not supposed to have earthquakes in Balona," I complain.

"Well, Tery Redlegs, occasional exceptions are said to prove the rule." He calls me Tery Redlegs only when he sees me wearing these stockings. He cocks his head at Richie who remains supine, his motorcycle still chugging now on its side, back wheel spinning.

Pastor Nim raises his voice. "You still alive there, Richie?" No answer.

Maybe Richie has met his Maker. I almost feel like smiling as Pastor Nim trots over to Richie and collapses his seven-foot frame down onto one knee and into an examination mode.

I rise and check myself for wounds. Finding none but a few scratches, I gravitate to Richie's location.

Pastor Nim squeezes Richie variously for broken bones. He performs as if he's done this sort of thing before. The way he moves around Richie reminds me that Nim was a marine hero in a terrible war and has likely seen a good many wounds. "You look like you're going to make it," says Pastor Nim finally. "Your motor is still working there, but it looks as if you'll have to invest in some cosmetics for it."

"I got a broken back," snivels Richie. "And my elbow hurts, too. Right here." He accuses the offending joint with his thumb. He glares at me and back at Pastor Nim. "I was just passing by the kid here, nice and smooth, when she whips her crappy old bike into me, like she wants to drive me right off of the road. So I had to swerve away to protect myself."

Richie seems to be making his voice shake.

"And then my tire blew or something. She had fell off of her crappy old bike there. See? Serves her right. You think I should sue? Sir?"

Richie has opened his eyes wide, fixing his face in what my brother describes as *the holy expression*. It's supposed to make the user look especially honest. As Richie has one green eye and one blue eye, the effect is at least remarkable if not startling, like his using "sir," but is not at all convincing as to Richie's honesty.

"Perhaps you've hit your head, Richie, and can't recall what really happened?" Pastor Nim moves as if to feel Richie's scalp, but Richie scuttles backwards. "It wasn't Tery trying to upset you. If anybody swerved, it was Tery trying to move away from you." Pastor Nim is smiling. "And it wasn't a blow-out that upset you, Richie. You got felled by a bolt from the blue. Seems appropriate," says Pastor Nim.

"What's that supposed to mean? Anyways, how do you know anything about it?"

"Well, I've been in conference in my office, but also noticing the world outside my window and monitoring the birds and the traffic." Pastor Nim raises his chin at the squirrels frolicking on his lawn. "And the squirrels, from time to time. And then you and Tery Redlegs here passed by. I saw what happened before the jolt, so I came out of my office to see if Tery was all right. My building creaked as you did your Evel Knievel act. We'll probably have another little quake pretty soon. They usually sing duets." Pastor Nim looks me over. "You look all in one patriotic piece, Tery. Are you?"

Patriotic. I think Pastor Nim is referring to my red stockings, white blouse, and blue skirt.

"Sure," I say. "No problem." I show my teeth. "Thanks," It's nice to have a sort of neighborhood watch going on most all the time in Balona. I mean, people don't always *do* anything when they see an accident or a fire, but in Balona at least they are said to *think* about doing something. Pastor Nim is an active doer.

"Well," says Pastor Nim, "I left a parishioner in the midst of a discussion, so I'd better get back in there now. Take care, Tery." He looks hard at Richie as he walks away. Even with a plastic foot, he seems not to allow himself to limp. "You, too, Richie."

Richie grumbles as he picks up his cycle. The machine coughs once and is silent. Richie tries unsuccessfully to start it, finally climbing off, letting it fall to the concrete, and kicking at the barrel. making a visible dent in it. He says a bad word.

"What's that running down your cheek?" I ask him, not exactly taunting, but curious.

"Probably blood. None of your business." He gives me a hard look. "And you leave the old man alone, hear?" he says. "I'm his legal hair, so everything he's got is mine." Richie raises the cycle, pushes it along the sidewalk toward his house, trying to wipe away tears as he goes.

I find that Hopalong is rideable, so I mount up and proceed to my appointment, not quite comforted in the knowledge that although Richie is a bully and a pig, he is also a vulnerable kid.

7

Pioneer Balonan details exciting life in the big city

I carry wounded Hopalong into the foyer of Jolly Times and lean him against a wall. Maybe my bike will escape damage here for a while, unless one of the residents longs for a fresh-air adventure and takes direct action. The rest home ambience is the same in early afternoon as it was in early evening, exuding the same smell, the residents in the same "recreational" configuration, rows of them nodding in the big room. Perhaps some of them never noticed the quake.

I escape the attention of Mr. Carbunzle who would likely have me take my bike outdoors. I make my way directly to Mr. Junior Kuhl's room. I enter carefully after tapping on the door but getting no answer.

Mr. Kuhl is again resting, so I seat myself in the metal chair. I pull up my stockings, noticing a place in the knitting where I need to do some repair work. I wait for Mr. Kuhl to awaken.

I consider myself a competent multi-tasker, so I meanwhile think about how I am going to put his story together to interest teen readers.

Mr. Kuhl makes gargling noises, snuffles, and passes some gas, almost quietly. I include this embarrassing fact because I am in my reportorial mode and want to present the man as he is. As Sheba suggests, he could have been quite handsome as a young man. He is still nice looking in a very old way.

At this moment he does not smell good.

I have just about decided to offer Mr. Kuhl to readers in Mr. Kuhl's own words, but "as told to Tery Ordway." In that way the reader will be able to think of Mr. Kuhl as the narrator of a sort of adventure story. I'll try to tease out the adventure parts and get him to emphasize those.

Mr. Kuhl opens his eyes.

"Mmmfff. You been watching me."

"I just got here, Mr. Kuhl. Did you feel the quake?"

He squints at me. "I wonder, do I snore? Daisy always said I snored, but I never could hear myself. Daisy herself snored, y'know."

"Daisy?"

"A Vegetable Runcible. Long blonde hair. Juicy young filly at first. Turned sour soon enough. Later on got to liking Grover a lot. Sort of snippy, even when she was young. She was already in Balona when we got over here from San Francisco."

Mr. Kuhl sighs deeply.

"She was in my fifth-grade class and she took to me right away. Followed me around the schoolyard. Always wanting bites of my sangwidges. All us rowdies used to sing the song that made her blush."

"Oh, I bet the song was 'Daisy, Daisy,' wasn't it?"

I have interrupted him again, but he isn't displeased. *"I'm half crazy, all for the love of you,* is the way it goes on. We'd sing 'Clementine,' too. That was a popular song, but not about Daisy. And 'I Been Working on the Railroad.' All popular songs. Everybody sang in those days. Not like nowadays when everybody shouts stuff you can't understand." Mr. Kuhl throws his head back and sings out:

> "I dream of Daisy
> with the light brown hair,
> Borne like a va-a-a-por
> on the summer air...."

Mr. Kuhl's singing voice is a high tenor, in-tune, and quite strong. So resonant, in fact, that shards of wallpaper vibrate visibly and my eardrums quiver as he sings *vapor.* The door bursts open and Mr. Carbunzle peers in. Kevin looks over Mr. Carbunzle's shoulder. Mr. Carbunzle appears irritated. Kevin is smiling.

Kevin says, "Is everything all right in here? Nobody having a heart attack? Only singing opera again?"

"I'm explaining old-timey tunes to this young person, so just get out now, Kevin. You, too, Wendel." Mr. Kuhl is polite but very firm. The intruders depart, Mr. Carbunzle shaking his head, Kevin chuckling.

"There's no music lovers around here, y'know. Oh, well, nowadays young folks don't sing music either. They just scream and shout. Did I already say that? Well, you can't actually hear a tune in modren music. Too bad. And you might be better off not hearing the words, if you catch my drift."

"We have a chorus at school and we sometimes sing the old songs. You mentioned Daisy."

"Told you already. Lived with that woman for sixty-odd years. Did make a fine sardine and onion sangwidge.

After a while she didn't love me no more. People are like that, y'know. First maybe they love you. Then maybe they don't. Then she passed over. Left me sitting there. Looking at her picture." He opens the front of his robe, feels about inside it, touching his neck and his chest. He is not wearing the silver locket today.

He speaks softly now.

"I look in the paper and see all over the TV women all gussied up. Why do they do that?" Mr. Kuhl points his slippered foot at the wall. "They sashay in that pointy-toe way, their lips red and shiny. To get theirselfs a man, that's why. And soon as they got him they're sagging around in the kitchen, and they quit pointing their toes, they don't sashay any more, lips all plain-colored. No more red stockings." Is he teasing me?

These remarks I cannot quote in my article, for the attitude Mr. Kuhl expresses would render him unsympathetic to at least fifty percent of the readers. I must tell him.

"I have to tell you something, Mr. Kuhl. You are expressing yourself in a manner that's known nowadays as sexist."

"That what they call it? Well, that's what it is, and it's a good name for it. Exactly what it is. You heard it from me." I think he winks at me. I cannot tell if he's serious or joking. "Of course, the men do it, too, y'know. Hair-combing and muscle-showing, big-talking.

And soon as they get their lady they plop theirselfs on the couch and scratch, drink beer, and grow a belly. Burping and belching. Romance? Scarcer than hen's teeth, yeah." Mr. Kuhl makes an effort to illustrate his argument with a burp, but nothing comes out. "Then the hair falls out. Of course, even as hairless wonders, we still talk big."

His facial expression is sly.

I say, "You were remembering your Daisy."

"Yeah. When I look at her, lots of stuff comes back." He gropes in the front of his robe. "I seem to have misplaced her."

"Well, I brought you something to help ease your starvation." I search in my backpack and find the sandwich.

"Oh, yeah. My starvation." Mr. Kuhl finally laughs aloud. He unwraps the peanut butter and banana sandwich and attacks it at once. "Mmm. Good." He looks at the ceiling. "The fat boy was here, too. I was taking me a nap, and there he was. Did he bring this sangwidge? No, you brought it. I wonder what he brought?" Mr. Kuhl nods off for a moment, jerks awake. "I got a good one, a knock-knock joke. You know about knock-knock jokes?"

"Yes, sir, I've heard a few of those."

He says, "Well, knock-knock."

I say, "Who's there?"

"Uh. I sort of forgot that one." Mr. Kuhl leans forward, as if ready to impart a confidence. "You know why the sailors can't play cards on their boat?"

"Why's that?"

"The captain is sitting on the deck." Mr. Kuhl doubles up at that. He stops laughing and looks hard at me. "You got a real pretty smile but you don't use it enough. You know that?"

I feel myself turn pink and say, "My brother tells me I have a dry wit."

"Careful it don't dry up on you before its time." Mr. Kuhl crinkles his eyes at me, showing me he's joking, and that I really ought to join in with his fun. "Y'know, my father told that one about the sailors. Told it a lot. One of his favorites of all time. Probably because it deals with cards. Deals with cards, get it? Never forget that one."

I wait a respectful interval and give Mr. Kuhl time to adjust his tongue and gums. Then I prompt: "Your Daisy was your wife."

"Yeah, you didn't need to remind me. We had three boys, but they came later, too. It was the horses I was fond of first. Before Balona. They was before Daisy. We didn't have a horse of our own before Balona. Not at first, anyways. Whenever we had to go somewheres in San Francisco, we walked. Or took a streetcar or a cablecar. Or Poppy took a cab. When I got me the job at the fire house, Grover was jealous, but he wasn't the go-getter I was."

"Grover was a fireman?"

"Grover was my brother. Him and me was born together. Twins, y'know, just like the babies, but I came out first. Poppy said I would always be a leader. So that's what I always tried to do."

"I've heard of you, Mr. Kuhl, but I never before heard of your brother."

"Well, that cinches it. Probably because Grover passed over a long time ago. Never worked at the fire house."

"He passed over in the fire?"

Mr. Junior Kuhl appears suddenly distressed, recovers quickly. "Brother Grover lasted through the fire. He was with us in Balona. But he passed over, an old man, right here in town.

"Wasn't a leader, though. I was the leader. Mayor a couple times. But I guess I should tell you about some exciting things, not politics. Politics is sometimes exciting, but not usually. Thing is, you got to be flexible in Balona politics. When you're flexible, you got to watch out you don't get threwn in jail." He chuckles. "Never got threwn in jail myself, even though I served as mayor."

"You're going to tell me about some exciting things."

82

"Sure, I can do that. Talk about exciting, let me tell you about what it was that woke me up. Woke me up out of a sound sleep." Mr. Kuhl then sits up straight and speaks out in quite a loud voice.

JUNIOR KUHL: But first, you need to know this:

> 'Twas the eighteenth of April
> in seventy-five.
> Hardly a man who's now alive
> remembers that famous day and year....

Well, that's Longfellow's poem, y'know. Henry Wadsworth Longfellow? And that's the poem about that grand midnight ride of Paul Revere. On the eighteenth of April in 1775. You know that poem? I learnt it in school. They teach you that in school? Shame on them. It's about a famous date you ought to learn. You can hear that horse galloping along under old Paul whilst you say the poem. [Mr. Kuhl drums horsely on the arm of his chair.]

> 'Twas the *EIGHT*eenth of *AP*ril
> in *SEV*enty-*FIVE*.
> *HARD*ly a *MAN* who's *NOW* a*LIVE*

But I'll tell you about another eighteenth of April.

This one was in nineteen-ought-six, and we was living upstairs in our flat in San Francisco. There was Mama and Poppy and Grover and me. [Mr. Kuhl counts off family on his fingers.] And little Billa and Sohny. And tiny little babies, Clarence and Esmeralda. Us bigger boys had our own little room where we slept. Along with Poppy's friends, Mr. Padmore and Mr. Slim. They worked at the same cardroom where Poppy was trying to make us rich.

In our bedroom we had two pictures of Indians on the wall. One of them with a feather headdress and sitting on a pony. The other one was just standing there. Shading his eyes with one hand and looking into the sunset. [Mr. Kuhl shades his eyes and simulates looking into sunsets in several directions.] I remember those pictures to this day. Always wisht I could've had them with me when we left for Balona. I looked at those pictures every night when I went to bed. And every morning when I woke up. Noble-looking fellers, those redmen. D-e-d now, of course.

Anyways, Mama and Poppy and tiny babies Clarence and Esmeralda slept in the room down the hall in the back. And in between, there was our sitting room where little Billa and little Sohny laid in their blankets nights. Each on his own end of the chesterfield. Scratchy piece of furniture. Itched you when you sat on it. Horsehair, y'know.

And down the hall in back was the kitchen and a fine-smelling pantry. Which I liked to sneak into.

The privy was down on the ground floor where all the families could use it. The ladies took turns mopping it out. It was a civilized inside water-flush privy, y'know. Not a one-holer in the backyard like we had in Sacramento when I was little. And later when we got to Balona. Don't look so surprised. Yep, a water-flush privy in San Francisco. We had a few conveniences back in those times. And there was a back porch where you could go out and look over at a little patch of the bay. When it wasn't too foggy.

Downstairs was Kling's Pharmaceuticals, which is what you used to call a drugstore in the old days. You could always breathe in the drugstore smell from out the window. [Mr. Kuhl breathes in, loudly.] And in the hall and on the stairs. I can smell it to this day.

Me and Grover had a bunk bed, where he had to sleep on the bottom. I got to climb a little ladder and sleep up on the top bunk, where you get most of the warm air. San

Francisco can be chilly at night, what with its fog. We always called the city San Francisco, where low types would say Frisco. [Mr. Kuhl squints his eyes at me, raises one bushy white eyebrow.] Kind of like low types today who will say Big Baloney instead of Balona High School.

Anyways, I had been in that top bunk all night long where for a couple of days it had been a lot warmer than usual. And now there was a faint light at the window, telling me it was almost time to get up. I usually woke up early, eager to get to my horses.

Suddenly my bed began to move. Not just wobbling back and forth, mind you. Like Grover ordinarily turning and tossing us. But up, up, up, and then down. [Mr. Kuhl thrashes about in his chair.] Like some giant was trying to skitter our bunk bed across the room. There was this roaring sound. Like a railroad train passing nearby. Only we had no train tracks nearby.

Of course Grover had to shriek. I just gritted my teeth, pretended I had a derringer like Poppy. I would plug that giant if he didn't stop it at once. [Mr. Kuhl demonstrates plugging behavior.] Mr. Padmore said a discouraging word or two. In the dim light I could see that he had been thrown right off of his cot. Right onto the floor.

That scene still makes my heart palputate to think about it now. You happen to have another sangwidge, by any chance? Oh. Too bad. Well, then, I think maybe I need to rest from the strain right now.

∾

And Mr. Junior Kuhl falls asleep right here and now. I want to prod him awake and find out about the giant and the skittering bed, but decide to let him rest. I can always come back later for the rest of his tall tale. It is beginning to sound like something by Mark Twain.

Looking at him with his chin on his chest, he snoring quietly now, I suddenly wonder how long Mr. Kuhl might continue to be strong enough to make himself available.

I hold my breath, leaving quietly as I can, thinking about how long Mr. Kuhl has already lived and how remarkable it is that he has been able to keep his spirits up in this place. "First they love you. Then they don't," he said. I wonder about that, but it sounds as if it might be too personal to quiz him about.

I wonder also about the odd disappearance of Mr. Kuhl's silver locket.

8

Eyewitness describes terrifying sounds and sights

I have transcribed my notes on brother Jack's computer, printed them on Jack's printer, fastened them together with a pink paperclip, and now present them to Sheba. We are not quite alone in the *Korndogger* classroom. Mr. Peralta has either not come in yet, or has already gone home.

In the back of the room the custodian is banging his mop against every chair and table leg. The stuff he is sweeping up smells like pencil shavings. The room is quite warm. Sheba appears to be in pain as she scans my several sheets.

"Too hoidy-toidy sounding. I can't use this stuff."

"These are notes, Sheba. This isn't the story. I'll write the story next, after I finish the interview. These notes are what guide me where to proceed in the composition."

Sheba keeps her pain active, twists her lips, rolls her eyes, sniffs, sighs. "Oh, yeah? I hope you know what you're doing. If you don't mind me saying so, I don't much like what you got here. What's this here about singing?"

"Mr. Kuhl sang a few phrases of an old song."

"Something from the Beatles?"

"Something probably earlier."

"Beatles might be interesting, except they're also old or dead. Either one. My Ma liked the Beatles, talks about 'em like they're in the next room. I myself prefer hip-hop." Sheba half-lowers her eyelids. "Your ma like the Beatles?" She touches her lips with her fingertip. "Oops. You don't got a ma. You're an orphan."

"I now have a complete family, Sheba, and have never been without my daddy. I'm hardly an orphan."

"I always heard when your ma dies, you're an orphan. Far as I'm concerned, you're an orphan. Poor thing." She sniffs. Sheba does not sound sympathetic. "Anyways, what about like some sex stuff from the old guy? Any sex stuff out of him yet?"

"Mr. Kuhl was married."

"Just married? Nothing else, like a girlfriend on the side? That could be interesting. But just marriage is like definitely not sex stuff. My ma will tell you all kinds of stuff about that."

"I guess it wouldn't be right for the *Korndogger*."

Sheba squints her eyes at me. "You being smart with me? I'm an older person and your superior with a philosophy of life, y'know. So don't try and get smart."

I say, "Simply an observation."

"I thought you'd like to know that my philosophy of life has went and told me to make up with my boyfriend."

"Isn't he the one who smacked you in the mouth?"

"So? I probably deserved it, what with me like saying a few comments about his mom." Obviously, we are discussing the eminent Richie Kuhl. "Anyways, he's always got a pocketful of cash, and he called me up and like told me he was sorry, but that he's got a hot nature." Sheba squints her eyes at me again. "See? Now there's got some sex appeal, where he like mentions his hot nature?"

The custodian, a heavy man with a gray mustache, is wearing grimy blue coveralls and a red Balona Bonkers baseball cap with the visor turned fashionably to the rear. He has been sweeping at the same pile of shavings for some time. "Richie Kuhl's a bad boy," he says. Sheba ignores him.

I say, "I guess I'm too young to appreciate Richie's charms." I don't intend to sound sarcastic, but maybe something peeps out along that line, for Sheba gives me another long look.

"It's not a matter of charms," she says. "It's he's like got charisma, which is different than charms, but something like it. He's got kids following him around. He knows guys. He knows how to do stuff, how to get stuff for free. He's got like all kind of connections." She takes a deep breath, her ample breasts rise, and she brushes invisible crumbs from her bosom. "And he likes me. Not everybody likes me, y'know."

She sniffs.

I withhold comment. Merely raise my eyebrows. "I'm going to pursue my interviewing with Mr. Kuhl, if that's okay with you."

"The old guy is Richie's great-grandpa, y'know."

I nod. "I thought there might be a connection."

"Richie told me he goes over there in the middle of the night, y'know, takes the old guy presents and stuff.

Surprises the old guy. Richie's got a good side to him that he like keeps hid so people won't take advantage."

"I see. Well, that's good news," I say. "Now, I'd better get on over there and resume my interview."

"Yeah, resume." Sheba appears not to approve of my manner of speech.

It would be interesting to witness Sheba and Richie head to head, their auras blending. I wonder what colors would predominate there.

The custodian stops his broom-banging, leans on the handle, raises his chin at me. "You gonna talk to old Junior Kuhl? Ask him about his horses. He's a horse-crazy old coot." He chuckles, wags his head, and attends to his unique broom work.

"If you don't mind me saying so, Mr. Serly here smokes pot in his closet down the hall. Everybody knows. He should talk about bad boys." Sheba gives Mr. Serly a hard look. "I'm gonna go home and get me some lunch and a nap. And maybe I'll watch 'The Young and the Ruthless' on our new 42-inch plasma TV. Maybe I'll meet up with Richie. He says he's went and got me a get-well present."

The all-call crackles near the ceiling at the head of the room. Someone breathes heavily, closely into the microphone, making the words difficult to understand. It seems to be the voice of Principal Croon: "I'm locking all the doors now, going home, so clear out all."

~

Balona summer days can be very, very hot, but the nights are often cool because of the breezes flowing over the huge expanse of delta marshland between the San Francisco Bay and our town. Mornings such as today's are usually very pleasant, so I usually wear my red stockings. But when I have finished pedaling to the Jolly Times Rest

Home today, I am perspiring as I lower my peanutbutter-sandwich-laden backback.

Leaving Hopalong at risk outside again, I enter, using my notebook as a fan to fend off the fumes. The recreation room is not quite as warm as a pizza oven at Mello Fello. Nearby, a woman looks up from her wheelchair. She seems to be very old. She smiles at me and quavers in a faint voice, "I wish I had one of those."

I tear out some pages, fold them, and hand her the makeshift fan.

Mr. Carbunzle races across the room. "You should just let staff give things to the residents, Miss. Otherwise they just get to expecting that everybody who comes in will give them a present." He gives the old woman a hard look. She smiles, fanning.

He growls, "They're just like children, y'know. We know how to make presents last, and we just give them to the more deserving residents. Ones that don't give us trouble."

"It was simply a fan, Mr. Carbunzle. I'd say she needs it. I'd say they all might do a bit better with a fan."

He ignores my suggestion. "Well, now she'll expect you to just give her something every time she sees you." Mr. Carbunzle frowns. "Just not a good idea. We really do know our business, y'know. Next time, just let us do it." Mr. Carbunzle's remark sounds like an order from a traffic policeman.

Mr. Kuhl is awake. He responds loudly to my rap on his door. "Hey, come on in." He waves me in, nodding his head, appearing livelier than at any previous time I've seen him. "You bring me something?" Perhaps Mr. Carbunzle has a point.

"Well, it's only another sandwich. I hope it helps."

Mr. Junior Kuhl reaches for the sandwich, tears off the paper, and digs right in. He speaks between bites. "They give me broccoli and hamburger for lunch. Hamburger was soupy, but no bread to sop up the gravy. And the broccoli was too tough to chew. Mmmm. This is pretty good. Did I ask you to marry me yet?"

"Mr. Kuhl, I'm too old for you."

Mr. Kuhl stops. His eyes get bigger. "Wha wha wha," he laughs loudly and slaps his knee. "I thought you was pretty dry, but by cracky, you got a sense of humor after all." He finishes his sandwich without delay.

I say, "You were about to tell me about the giant."

"What giant was that?"

"The one in your room that skittered your bed and made Grover shriek and Mr. Padmore say a discouraging word."

"I said all that, did I? Well, it wasn't exactly a giant. Not the kind you're familiar with. You ever hear of the Great Quake?"

I wag my head. I'd heard of quakes in San Francisco and around Los Angeles and in foreign lands. I remembered hearing about the quake that broke the San Francisco Bay Bridge a few years ago. That one was pretty big. It smashed concrete overpasses and squashed cars on the Oakland freeway and dumped people into the bay, but I never heard of a big one closer to home. Not a really, really *great* quake.

MR. KUHL: Take it from me, the Great Quake of nineteen-ought-six was a big one. I got me up off of the floor back then. I looked at the window. It wasn't square any more. It was shoved out of shape, almost like a triangle. The window glass was all gone. Mr. Padmore was complaining that he had stepped on glass and his feet was cut.

And our Indians fell in their frames down to the floor. And the room kept moving, and the sounds? You could hear crackling and crumbling sounds. And that big sound like a freight train going by right next door. Only it wasn't the freight train. It was our building breaking up. Falling apart.

And you could hear Poppy shouting something. And Grover wouldn't shut up until I smacked him one on the arm. Then he shut up. And we grabbed up our overalls and shoes and ran downstairs. Banging our naked selfs against the walls as we went. Since the quake was going on and on, throwing us off-balance.

Down in the street, the sun wasn't quite up yet, but the street was full of part-naked people trying to dodge flying bricks. Men hollering. Women screaming. Dogs barking and horses whinnying. Some of them gone scared wild, almost.

We could hear bells all over. Church bells bonging by theirselfs. Fire whistles going off, and buildings falling apart. Bricks lofting into the street. A woman on her knees in the gravel and broken glass singing a church hymn. A rich person in an automobile weaving his noisy crooked path around glass and bricks. Hollering at folks to get out of his way. Pounding on his klaxon. Almost running over people. I tell you, it was crazy.

Also scary.

Then Poppy finally found his way down the stairs. Practically carrying Mama. Followed by Billa and Sohny. Both little ones shrieking like they'd been stuck. Mama was holding her head. Something had fallen on her and made her bleed a lot. She was groaning up a storm.

At this time the ground had stopped the big shaking and rolling. The sun was probably coming up. Only you couldn't exactly see the sun on account of the fog ballooning up faster than the sun. San Francisco fog does that, y'know. First, it's not there. All of a sudden, there it comes, thick as a chunk of sour French bread. The shaking and quaking was maybe only a few minutes. The buildings falling down. But it seemed like hours.

Then the shaking stopped, and it got quiet all at once.

TERY: You say your building was falling down? Did you say that? That your house was falling down?

MR. KUHL: Not only falling down. Collapsed up and fell down. Right into Kling's Pharmaceuticals. Glass all over the street. Mr. Padmore's feet wasn't the only ones cut up. Mr. Slim got cut, too, and more of our neighbors.

"Earthquake," Poppy explained. His voice was shaking. "That's what you just had."

I had felt a few little shakes before, but never felt a big one like that. Decided I didn't want to feel another one for a while.

Actually, there was little usual-type quakes after that for a few days. Another big one later in the morning that I'll tell you about maybe later, if I'm still alive and kicking. But after the first big rocker, nobody paid a whole lot of mind to the little ones. Besides, by then we had went to the cemetery.

Speaking of little ones, me and Grover and Mr. Padmore and Mr. Slim had left our place in a huge big hurry. Poppy had practically carried Mama downstairs in such a great pickle, followed by two screaming kids, that we'd left the babies in their little boxbed upstairs. Still upstairs, which wasn't exactly upstairs any more.

At the time, nobody seemed to notice about the little babies not being with us. All of us happy to be in one piece. Poppy was worried about Mama's bleeding head and the noise she was making about it. I felt like I might like to hug Poppy and Mama. But I held off, being manly. Besides, I had to strap up my overalls, the old good kind where you snap the straps over your shoulders to the bib.

I also figured if I tried to hug Mama I would get blood on me from her head, which Poppy was wrapping up with a couple of rags tore off the shirttail of his long-johns top. Poppy had his derringer coat and pants on. But he didn't have a shirt on. He was barefoot. Mr. Padmore and Mr. Slim was barefoot, too, and went off looking for anything to wear on their feet.

Neighbors from our building were doing a lot of hollering. Some had got out in time. Some I guess were stuck in the rubble. You could hear coughing and swearing and screaming. People were running around in the street like chickens with their heads cut off.

Then the fire started.

"It's burning, the building's burning." some lady was shouting, which was pretty obvious, because of the orange flames shooting out of where the big downstairs window of Kling's Pharmaceuticals used to be.

It looked to me like the fire had started there. Down in the basement. That's where the big flames were coming from. The fire was spreading fast.

"Get the fire department over here," somebody else yelled. I volunteered to run down to rouse the boys at my engine house. So I slipped on my shoes and did just that. Trouble is, when I got to where the firehouse was, they was gone, horses and all. Later, I found out they'd been on a fire call early that morning. They had missed having their firehouse collapse down on them. Which it would have done, since the firehouse now was just a huge big pile of bricks.

This was a miserable feeling, since I didn't know what else to do. Except go for my firemen. Which I had went and done. I felt sort of heroic and stupid at the same time. I raced back to our place with the news. But, lo and behold, my firemen had got there already from the other direction.

They couldn't bring the engine up to the place. Since there was so much rubble and people and stuff in our street. "We run out of water anyways," went Mr. Jerry Williams, a big hoseman with a prizefighter's nose. He was always joking you with a big smile. Not this time. "No water, so we'll throw some sand on it," he said.

And the firemen went and took shovels. Got some sand from where there was a building going up next door. Wore theirselfs out running back and forth, throwing sand at the fire.

But it was too late.

The fire was already too big. The flames turned from brown to orange. To yellow to blue. That means they got hotter and hotter. We all had to move back. People hollering. Flames crackling.

Then is when the screaming for real started. We could hear little Esmeralda and little Clarence especially loud. I think probably it was them, but there was lots of other screaming from little voices and big voices. Our neighbors had kids, too.

Most of the screaming came from people who just didn't get out of there in time. But there was screaming and hollering from relatives who had went and got theirselfs out first.

Mama was all for climbing into that rubbledy hot fire to try and rescue them. But the firemen pushed her and Poppy back. "You will die in there, lady, and we can't let you do that." That is what Hoseman Williams hollered at Mama and Poppy. He wasn't joking us, neither.

So Poppy held Mama tight, and they both stood gasping and crying with the rest of us. Until the fire eating our building sort of went up to blue and yellow leaping flames and then down to brown and smelly smoke and ashes. We couldn't stand there for long, since the buildings next door and across the street were on fire and burning like mad, too. Like a huge big celebration bonfire.

What we did do was drag ourselfs up the street. Over a few blocks to the cemetery where the fire couldn't burn any buildings. Most of the houses, big apartment houses in our neighborhood, were fallen down in pieces. We could see our block start to go up in flames.

What else could we do?

The smoke was thick everywhere. You could hear the bells still clanging on fire engines. Over on another corner a bunch of men was galloping in and out of Zeke's Place. They served beer and liquor there. But now the whole front of the building was down on the street. It looked like the men was carrying bottles. Or rolling barrels and running off in all directions. But pretty soon that place caught on fire, too.

The men stopped racing in and out. I watched the flames. Heard the sounds of walls tumbling, crashing down. People all around us either snuffling and weeping and screaming. Or else sort of breathing choppy. Mama and Poppy just sat on a gravestone and looked at the ground. Not talking. Mama would suck in a loud shaky breath every once and a while.

I wondered what it would be like to feel the flames coming for you. Close up, like my baby sister and brother must have felt.

[Mr. Kuhl takes a long breath and sighs.]
In the middle of the night, I still wonder about it.

~

I leave Mr. Kuhl quietly.

Homeward bound, I try to keep my mind occupied with thoughts of how best to organize my material. Easier to think about organization and other trivia than about burning babies.

9

Elder describes second temblor in shocking detail

Mr. Junior Kuhl appears especially haggard when I next visit. He also has a bruise around, under, and beside one eye, as if he has fallen against something hard, like a door frame.

Perhaps in going to his bathroom he had been uneasy on his feet and had fallen.

He keeps touching the brownish bruise, and I suggest aloud that maybe he has a headache or a toothache.

"I been mugged. Probably meant to shanghai me."

"You mean attacked? Someone attacked you?"

"Two big guys with guns. Come in here in the middle of the night. Beat me up with a lead pipe. One of 'em had a blackjack."

As he speaks, he shifts his gaze to my chin, then to my ears, one at a time. "They was looking for jewels. I told 'em I don't got jewels. But they looked everywhere anyways. Then they beat me up."

"I see. Well, I guess you've reported it."

"Don't do no good to do that. Those guys are wraiths, y'know. Masked-up in black. They disappear into the dark of the night. Like The Shadow or The Prince of Darkness."

"Wraiths?" I'm not sure I've heard the word correctly.

"Like ghosts. You can't hear when they come in. It's so quiet, y'know. And then they sort of float away in the mist. I don't mind all that much, since I'm the sort that don't feel much pain. And I don't got any jewels left. Now, old Kon Chaud down the hall there. He's got jewels and cash hid under his mattress. Probably I ought to work up enough spit to go down there and warn him." Mr. Kuhl nods off for a while.

I suspect that Mr. Junior Kuhl was at one time famous for telling tall tales. Tall-tale-telling is a sport in Balona, celebrated especially, I'm told, at Ned's Sportsbar. Our neighbor, Mr. Junior Kuhl's grandson, Mr. Kenworth Kuhl, is famous for his tall tales. Perhaps that talent runs in the family.

I prod, "Mr. Kuhl, are you awake or asleep?"

MR. KUHL: Did I say about the cemetery? I did? Well, when we got there, Poppy was practically carrying Mama. She was still snuffling and looking at the ground. Her feet bottoms were bloody. That's what Poppy had been looking at.

TERY: I suppose she was grieving for her little ones.

MR. KUHL: That's not the point of my story. I mean, we was all grieving, more or less. When you lose a baby, your ma is going to grieve. Probably your dad, too, some. When you lose a pair of babies, like Mama did, it's all the

100

worst. But brothers and sisters never really get to know little babies. Unless they got to carry the kid around and wipe up after it. So a baby's just another noise and a smell in the house. A noise that gets all the attention. So, when it passes over, you're sort of sad. But you say to yourself, Well, life goes on.

I thought for a while that I should have ran back into that burning building, y'know. Rescued those little tykes. Get celebrated as a hero. Enjoy the relief of my parents. But I just stood there like a stick. Like everybody else. I don't really think about it any more. Of course. Not all that much.

Anyways, there we was in the cemetery. Sitting on gravestones. Getting our butts chilled. The wind in San Francisco usually comes off of the ocean. From the west, y'know. But that day for some reason, it shifted and was coming from the east. Off of the land beyond the bay. The wind seemed to be pushing the fire in front of it, into the city. But the cemetery was a place where you didn't have any fire burning. Or buildings falling on you.

And at least in the cemetery you didn't have rats running all over. The way they were doing in the streets. Too many for a few cats and dogs to take care of. I don't know where all those rats went afterwards. I figure they had all came out of the houses and other buildings to escape the quake and fire.

Poppy kept looking at Mama's feet, bare and bloody, like his own, where he had somehow forgot to climb into his boots in all the excitement. Anyways, he took off his derringer coat. You could see he also had forgot to put on his shirt. Only his long-johns top to fend off the fog.

With his leg knife he cut the sleeves off of his fine coat up to the elbows. So when he put the coat back on, there was his long-john sleeves peeping out of where his coat sleeves used to be. His hairy belly showing above his belt, where he had cut off his long-johns shirtbottom to tie up Mama's bleeding head.

Quite a sight. Me and Grover couldn't help but to chuckle over that.

Poppy told me to give him the laces out of my shoes. He could've took Grover's shoelaces, but I was right near. He pulled one of the pieces of coat-sleeve over each of Mama's poor sore feet. Folded each sleeve-piece up. Then he tied a shoelace around each one. Made sort of a pair of shoes for her. Funny looking, but at least soft and warm. She could walk a ways in those new shoes.

That sacrifice of my shoelaces was fine with me. Except it took me quite a while to find another set. Which I found in shoes that somebody had lost out in the street. I had to shuffle my feet to get anywhere. Until I found those old laces.

You'd expect a lot of noise from a cemetery full of live people. But no, it was quiet as a churchmouse there. Where it was real noisy was in the streets nearby. A lot of people was going fast as they could. Through the rubble and smoke down to Market Street. Poppy said it looked to him like they was probably headed for the Ferry Building down at the end of Market.

The whole shebang was trying to get across the bay and out of town. Not only the people made noise. The fire was making plenty of that itself. And then we heard huge big booms from down in the business district. "I bet they're dynamiting," went Poppy. Explaining that they were starving the fires, probably.

Blowing up buildings that would otherwise give the flames something to eat.

A few other people ran around like the rats, from street to street, too. They weren't going to Market Street. They were going into what was left of stores and houses. Taking stuff that didn't belong to them. Did you think it was only evil men that was doing that? Nice females would probably think that. Well, you'd be mistaken if you thought that. It looked to me like as many females as men running into ruined houses and taking stuff that didn't belong to them. Stuffing things into bushel baskets and burlap sacks. Carrying them off.

"Them's looters," said Poppy. "'Nobody owns this any more,' they will tell you, 'so we'll just take it over.' But that's wrong. That's looting, and looters are plain thieves. And when the police come, those looters'll get threwn in jail." Which is almost what happened. But not quite, since what happened later down on Market Street was a dang sight worst for some of those looters.

We saw a beat-up-looking old lady, probably not a looter, pushing a sewing machine down the street. The old-timey kind fashionable in those days. Where it has wheels the size of a yo-yo and a big metal foot-pedal to make the needle go up and down. Mama used to sew us shirts with one of them at Mrs. Riley's place downstairs. The old lady in the street was crying since she didn't have nothing but that machine to call her own property. And the sewing machine's tiny wheels kept hitting against bricks and rocks. And she kept trying to push it along anyways.

"We should get ourselfs across the bay, too," cried Mama, "before we all die." Poppy patted her on the shoulder. Told her not to cry, and that he'd go and take care of us, never mind. He pulled out his beautiful old watch that his own father gave him. Gold with a genuine green leather fob. Did I already say that? The fob is what's attached to the stem there. You pull on it to get it out of your vest pocket. Poppy wasn't wearing his vest. So he pulled it out of the pocket of his derringer coat.

"It's nigh onto eight o'clock already," he said, looking at the sky. We'd been sitting in the cemetery for pretty near two hours already. The sun was all up. The sky was blue in places already. But mixed with fog and a whole lot of black and white smoke. It was going to be a nice spring day, if you could call it nice. Under the circumstances.

So we decided to go down to Market Street and see what was up. How we could best get on one of those ferryboats. Actually, all of us didn't go down to Market Street to see what was going on. The little ones crying and Mama's feet hurting. All of us hungry, me especially.

So me and Poppy took off to see what could be done.

TERY: [Interrupting again.] Did Grover go with you?

MR. KUHL: Grover was whining and carrying on. Not manly at all. Poppy told him he had to stay and see after Mama and the little ones. That made Grover whine even more. But Poppy gave him a hard look, and that shut him up. Poppy had a real fine hard look which he said he had picked up from a gunfighter when still a youth up in Gold Hill. Poppy had refined it all this time, and could do it real nice even when he wasn't vexed about something. See?

[Mr. Kuhl demonstrates the hard look, a facial expression that seems to reveal Mr. Kuhl suffering severe pain.] So when Poppy give you his hard look, you didn't argue him at all.

Truth to tell, I never could get it quite right.

Anyways, me and Poppy took off the long way down Van Ness Avenue, to avoid big fires, and took us past the new city hall and post office. Now there was a sight. Brand new buildings, both of them, fell-down in huge pieces.

And they had laid out dead bodies across the street in the park. Looked like hundreds. People killed by falling stuff and electricity in fell-down wires. And there was small fires starting up everywhere. Mostly from the busted gas mains.

You see, the water mains had also busted from quaking. And there wasn't no water pressure. So the poor firemen had to chop down stuff and throw sand on whatever looked like you had a chance to put out its fire. The fire system just wasn't working any more. Except by hard sweat. Harder than usual, for sure.

What was still working was the looters.

Did I mention the looters? I did?

You could see small groups of men—and women, too—going from one place to another. Running in and carrying out whatever they could manage: food things, furniture, a birdcage with a bird in it, all kinds of stuff. I was thinking I might be a looter for a good liverwurst sangwidge on brown bread with lots of butter. But I felt guilty right away for the thought. Me and Poppy stopped there in the mist of the smoke and fire. Looking at all this activity. Wagging our heads we was so surprised. Disappointed at the evildoing.

Then we saw some men putting up posters, yellow pieces of paper with printing. So we went over and took a look at where a poster was tacked to a pole. I was able to read it easy, since I learnt to read early in life. The poster was from Mayor Schmitz.

"It's a name like Kuhl," went Poppy, "A good name." Mayor Schmitz said on his poster that anybody who looted would be persecuted. But the posters didn't seem to bother the looters much at the time. Just then came a sight for sore eyes.

Coming down from over the hill was the U. S. Army. Lots of soldiers, marching as to war. A big soldier with a wide mustache on his lip, going on before. The soldiers had guns. "Those are bayonets," Poppy explained, which meant that glistening at the end of each gun was a sword stuck on it so you could poke with it.

Of course, from my studies I already knew what a bayonet was. But I didn't let on that I already knew. Poppy always felt good telling me manly stuff. But those soldiers looked so grand that I thought for a minute about joining the army. Lucky I never did.

The soldiers were still in their fine blue winter uniforms. Brass buttons down their fronts. On their cuffs. And ribbons on their hats. Those fellers spread out in smaller groups, going from block to block. Trying to stay out of the way of the firemen who had a tough enough job already fighting flames without being stuck accidentally with a bayonet.

Then came something I won't forget. There was worst to come, but this was the first time I ever saw it happen. Just as some soldiers trotted by, a bunch of looters came out of what was left of a jeweler's place. Carrying boxes and sacks, probably jewels.

"Stop and stand right where you are," yelled a chief soldier at the first looter.

"Hah," went the first looter with an armful of loot, probably jewels. He hared off, running.

The soldier stuck his rifle out, aimed it, and shot the looter, right in the back. He fell down, probably dead. His loot scattered in the cobbles and dirt of the street. The other looters dropped their booty. Scattered like rats.

The soldiers paid no attention to the shot body or the jewels in the dirt. Stepped over it. Marched off fast, mostly in step, trotting down the street, their eyes peeled for other evildoers. That was some lesson. I resolved never to become a looter. Even though tempted from time to time. Sorely tempted, you might say.

Then came something even worst. We went picking our way down the middle of Market Street. Through stones and bricks. Back towards the Ferry Building. By this time, Poppy had on a pair of boots he had found in a box abandoned outside a store on Van Ness. Poppy wasn't limping much. And I had found me those laces, so I wasn't shuffling any more, either.

On the middle of the street I had also found an empty suitcase. Not very huge. Brown and with fine leather straps around it. Poppy let me keep it, since I mentioned it was obviously abandoned and could come in handy if we found some food. "Good thinking," he said.

Except I had to carry it. But that wasn't the worst part.

We stepped over streetcar tracks. The quake had bent those iron rails crooked, until some of them were flat but twisted. Others were sticking up a couple feet from level.

And we had to go around huge big holes in the street. Where you could see that one of those holes was maybe ten feet deep. Water in the bottom of it. Once and a while we would have to jump out of the way of an automobile. Or a horse running without harness, saddle, or rider. But right there on the south side of the street, with people rushing by us, all going towards the Ferry Building all the way down at the end of the street, right there in the rubble lay the body of a woman. And standing over her was a scruffy-looking man brandishing a knife.

The woman had both her ankles showing. So that meant she must be passed over. D-e-d. Her head was stove in. Quite a few bodies were there in the rubble. I felt like throwing up, except I hadn't no breakfast to throw up. But you could see this lady had jewels on and rings on her fingers. It looked to me and Poppy that this scruffy feller was trying to steal her jewels.

"You, there," hollered Poppy in his loudest voice, which was pretty loud. Even when he got old. "Leave off brandishing that knife. Let that woman be." A few people stopped to watch. People will always stop to watch.

"Shut yer cake-hole," went the scruffy man. "I'm just getting something that she won't need no more." And he started to cut off the woman's finger to get to her rings.

Behind my right ear came a huge loud explosion.

I practically jumped out of my skin from the shock of it all.

Holding my ear, I turned and there was a policeman in a blue uniform and a tall hat, with his huge big blue revolver in his hand. The pistol was still smoking, and he blew his breath on it as he stuffed it back into its holster. My head was ringing from the sound. And I turned back towards the scruffy man with the knife. He wasn't cutting anything now. He was flat on his back, next to the dead woman.

Not moving. His ankles was showing, too.

The policeman said not a word. Just walked on. The crowd began moving again. I couldn't hear Poppy when he was trying to get me to move on, too. I was leaning over and actually throwing up, even without breakfast.

You see death on the TV nowadays, but it's not like the real thing. The real thing will make you throw up. Poppy jerked me by the sleeve, me wiping my mouth on my other sleeve. And we began going with the crowd down Market Street. Me still carrying my suitcase.

Poppy said, "I'm sorry you had to see that, Junior."

But even that was not the worst part.

When we got almost to the Ferry Building there was a huge big crowd already there. People hollering and trying to shove their way forward. But there was not only policemen holding the crowd back, there was soldiers, too. So the crowd was mostly just making noise.

Poppy asked a skinny man nearby, "When will the ferries start running?"

"Who knows?" went the skinny man. "Some of them ferries ain't even in their slips. Them and a lot of ships stayed out in the bay. Just to keep us from getting out of here." Lots of people around us agreed and grumbled and mumbled.

One of the crowd mentioned a huge big tidal wave was always a possible partner with an earthquake. Probably that's why the ships were not in port.

"What's a tidal wave?" I said to Poppy. "Are we gonna get drowned by one of them things?"

"If we do, we'll have a lot of company." Everybody around us laughed. Sort of nervously. Poppy was a cool customer, all right. Probably came with poker playing. He never did answer my question, though. Maybe he didn't exactly know how to say what a tidal wave is. That's what you call a *technique,* y'know.

I have found that technique to be useful when you're dealing with the young. You change the subject. Just don't answer the question.

Finally, a man way down in front hollered through a megaphone — that's an old-time bull-horn, a big hollow cone where you holler into the small end of it. Makes your voice sound bigger. I guess he was standing on a box since you could see him. As well as his megaphone.

"There's no ferry until 10:30 this morning, precise. And then we'll have a drawring for who gets on." He stopped and put down his megaphone. Turned his head around so he could give everybody a hard look. "Anybody tries to crash that line will be shot." The crowd that had been muttering through the man's speech suddenly became quiet as a churchmouse. You could hear the stomach on the feller next to us gurgling. Mine was gurgling, too.

And then the smell of the fire started up again and the noise of the blasting and the crashing of buildings and the shouts of firemen and army men and policemen.

Then the man leaped up on his box again. Raised up his megaphone. Everybody still hanging around got quiet. "Man here says that soon as they get some new track laid, the Southern Pacific right over there at Third and Townsend will be starting up some trains out of town."

A voice shouted: "What if your only cash is all back under a hunnert feet of rubble and ashes?"

"Well, you could probably get on a train if you looked poor enough—and was a weakling, wasn't able-bodied. The railroad people said able-bodied men should ought to stick around and help out."

We all looked down at the streetcar tracks, bent and twisted. We thought about how railroad tracks might be heavier than streetcar tracks, and not so bent and twisted. Poppy hollered, "How long you figure they'll be repairing the tracks?"

"I'm not a railroad man. How should I know? Maybe a day. Maybe an hour. Who knows? If you can get down a ways towards Burlingame, the man here says there's tracks already in good shape and a train that'll take you to San Jose and south. Tickets are said to be free down there. And if you need something to eat, man here says they've set up a soup kitchen over on Mission there, a couple blocks."

110

"That's the way to go," said a feller nearby, and turned around and left on the run.

A lot of people turned right around and followed him.

"Are we gonna go over to Third and Townsend and get on a train, Poppy?"

"As anybody can plainly see, I'm able-bodied, not a weakling. They won't let me on a train. Besides, we're not going anywheres without the rest of our family."

"Oh. Well, are we going down to Burlingame and get on the train and go to San Jose, Poppy?"

"Burlingame's a good fifteen miles away. Too far for your poor mama's feet to walk." Poppy sighed.

"And San Jose's a lot farther. And they probably got problems there, too. No, we're gonna sweat it out here in the city for the rest of the day. Whilst I think some about what to do. Meantime, we'll go over to Mission Street. Get us a bite to eat."

"Are we gonna get us a drawring and get on the ferry at 10:30 precise, Poppy?"

"No drawring for us. We'll never get up to your mama and back again by 10:30, precise or not. So we'll sweat it out here. Whilst I think some about what to do. Like I already said." Poppy gave me a sort of hard look. But not real hard. [Mr. Kuhl demonstrates his Poppy's not-real-hard look: A minor headache.]

TERY: People were waiting around for ferry-boats, so I'm guessing the bridges were all down.

MR. KUHL: What bridges? No bridges built yet. Not a one. This was a hundred years ago, girl.

Anyways, right then the ground started to jump and roar, just like before. People were screaming and running. What bricks were still stuck on buildings still standing came flying down. Along with window glass left over from

111

the first big quake. More electric poles bending and lines falling every which way. Another streetcar rail popped itself up in front of us, and a gas line leaped up out of the ground across the street. Made a huge big flame that the firemen started to throw sand on right away. But the gas gasped its last right away. No pressure.

The quake seemed to last forever. Up and down and sideways. We got down on our hands and knees since we couldn't stand up. People fell down, like before. Noise like you wouldn't believe. Dust to choke the breath right out of you. And screaming. Seemed like everybody was screaming. I think even I screamed once or twice. More rats scampering and squealing.

Poppy took his bandana out of his derringer coat, folded it into a triangle. Tied it around my mouth. Like a Mexican bandido. I could breathe without coughing. But Poppy couldn't.

I felt bad for Poppy, who did that heroic deed for his beloved oldest son.

TERY: [Mr. Kuhl pauses and wipes his eyes. I get the idea that he is ending the session, so I rise.]

MR. KUHL: You got to go already? Well, don't forget to bring me something. Maybe something cool to drink. When I think about it, I get thirsty as a camel on the desert.

TERY: When you think about. . .?

MR. KUHL: The shaking stopped after a while. And we thought we could walk and not fall down. I was so thirsty my throat was on fire. So I grabbed onto Poppy's hand. Pulled him along to where the buildings had already fell every which way. Where there wasn't bricks flying. There was still a lot of smoke, though. Maybe we could find us some water, I thought.

I kept on thinking to myself how just yesterday Mama had punished me for blowing bubbles in my milk with my red souvenir straw from Chinatown. Made me sit under the kitchen table for an hour. "Like a dog," she said. Grover blew bubbles in his milk, too, but she didn't punish him.

Hundred years ago and I still think about that.

Anyways, I was thirsty as all get out, and the fires wasn't going anywhere but towards us.

So go ahead and leave, girl.

But [Mr. Kuhl smacks his lips.] don't forget to bring back something wet.

10

San Francisco burned a century ago. Balona fire raged last night

The *Korndogger* classroom is a zoo. Kids talking about the latest in the string of mysterious Balona fires. A vacant house down on Seventh Avenue, not far from the King Korndog plant burned to the ground last night. The burn smell is all over Balona this morning, and *Korndogger* kids are wondering aloud about procedures of the famous Balona Volunteer Fire Brigade.

Although the fire fighters themselves are admirable and often heroic when they give themselves a chance, the fire department is a common target for homeowner complaint, and sometimes rightly so.

The Fire Center is a phone located sometimes at Kute Kurls & Nails and sometimes at Mr. Kenworth Burnross's law office. One has to know which number is "live" in order to get through to the volunteer dispatcher on duty. Or else one has to punch in both numbers, if those numbers can be remembered in the excitement of the moment.

And, even if you make the connection, the dispatcher may be sound asleep and hard to wake or be having a beer at Ned's Sportsbar or engaged in a line or two at Frings Bowls instead of waiting faithfully at his post by the phone.

So getting the news about a fire to the volunteer firemen — they're all men — is often chancey. To effect this process at night we are instructed in school, from first grade on up, that if we detect any kind of blaze to run out in the street and yell "fire." We are informed that somebody in the neighborhood is probably a volunteer fireman and will wake up the rest of the company.

The system makes for a rather slowly operating team, and very often a building that catches fire at night simply burns to the ground before the firefighters arrive. Following a tradition known throughout Chaud County, the firefighters always stop to haul several cases of Valley Brew onto the engine before they depart for the site of a fire. Fire fighting is invariably a hot and sweaty business requiring volumes of liquid replenishment, we are told.

I suggest aloud, "Maybe somebody ought to write a story about how a few women might better serve the department as dispatchers." I realize immediately from the expressions on the faces of the *Korndogger* staff that perhaps I should keep my mouth shut.

But Sheba appears interested. "Why's that?"

"Well, I'll bet they could get one of the regulars at Kute Kurls & Nails to volunteer. I've been told that the male volunteers there say they can't stand the smell or the noise and so frequently go down the street for a beer. Or two. Or more."

I chuckle. Mr. Peralta chuckles and nods his agreement, as members of my family would have done. None of the other students laugh.

"If you don't mind me saying so, my ma runs Kute Kurls & Nails. Changing it's not in her philosophy of life."

"My dad's chief of the volunteers. He wouldn't go for it at all." This is a surprise. The speaker is Franky Floom, son of Fire Captain Frank Floom. I recognized Franky, but hadn't considered his ancestry when I made my smart-mouth remark.

I shuffle papers to hide my embarrassment.

Mr. Peralta changes the subject. "How's your story progressing, Tery?"

I take a long breath and center myself the way my Master Tri describes. "I already have far too much material for one story. And I think there's a lot more to come. Mr. Junior Kuhl's an interesting man. Maybe I could write a series about his life?"

"Well, we're able to print only one *Korndogger* issue, you remember. So this one has to show them we're good."

"Oh. True. I forgot."

Mr. Peralta laughs. "I was once told that it's impossible for Tery Ordway to forget anything."

"Just goes to show, nobody's perfect." I correct the sagging of my stockings to further illustrate the fact that I'm not perfect.

"Well, I'll put in a word for you with Patrick Preene. Perhaps your series could be published in the *Courier*. Of course, we'll need a much shorter version for the *Korndogger*, an extract probably."

"Sure," I say. "If I can finish up with Mr. Junior Kuhl soon, I can have the story for you early next week.."

"Sounds good." Mr. Peralta nods.

Sheba intrudes. "Not good enough. I thought you're gonna give your trash to me to edit, eksedra." Her tone conveys resentment and pain.

"I was using the word you in its plural sense."

I should know better than to slip into my habitually sesquipedalian mode. "Of course my story goes to you to edit." I think a second and add, "Naturally, I'll present it in a form that's well-finished so you won't have to spend much time working over trash. Spare you the pain of that labor."

"Well. Yeah." Sheba sniffs, but becomes friendlier, comes closer and seats herself across from me at the small work table. No other student is nearby. Sheba leans in confidentially. "You know about the fire last night?"

"I didn't pay attention to the siren last night, but you can smell the results of the fire all over town today."

"Richie was there, y'know. He was the one went out in the middle of Seventh Avenue and hollered 'fire,' only nobody called the firemen, I guess. Richie called me up in the middle of the night and told me confidentially all about it, about how Zack Burnross did it. 'But don't tell anybody I said so,' Richie went."

I couldn't believe my ears. "I don't understand. You say Zachary did what?"

"Zack Burnross set the fire. Richie says it's a simple trick to do. You just get a little can of gasoline to sprinkle around and a book of paper matches, and then you like fold the matchbook and light one of the matches. And after a while all the matches like blow up and fire off the gasoline where it like starts burning the house down, and you have already went away from the scene."

I say, "I've heard that a journalist has to be sure of all the facts before accusing someone of a crime." I wonder how Richie happened to be at the origin of the fire in the middle of the night, but I don't ask the question.

"Well, Richie knows all about facts like that. It's part of his philosophy of life to know stuff. So I believe him. Anyways, if you don't mind me saying so, Zack Burnross is rich, and he's a wimp and a wuss." Sheba then changes the subject almost without taking a breath. "You said you don't know karate?"

"Never studied it. Know it only from TV."

"Richie knows karate. He's a blackbelt. Guys fear his wrath and his fist of death."

She sniffs.

I utter only a "Mmm-hmm," without rolling my eyes.

If Richie knows karate or anything requiring diligent study and prolonged sweaty activity, then pigs can fly. I think that some people may lie about personal achievements that they believe will never be tested.

"I figure what with your red leg-warmers there you're too cold to have a philosophy of life, right?"

"Oh, no," I say. "I operate on some principles."

"Yeah? Like what?"

"Well, it's What will be, will be. Accept what is. Do your best. Enjoy what is enjoyable. And this, too, shall pass."

"Oh." Sheba shrugs, frowns, twitches her head as if to clear it. She does not share her own philosophy of life. "I like told you already about my great boyfriend, right?"

I keep my attention focused on my notes.

She lowers her voice. "You're twelve, so even if you've got leg-warmers on a hot day and a old bike and a weird philosophy of life, you probably had sex already, right?"

I can feel my cheeks become pink, my lips tighten. Sex is everywhere, but it's something I try not to think about all the time. I say, "I don't care to discuss stuff like that."

"Yeah. So you haven't or you'd be bragging on it. Well, the news about me and my boyfriend, if you haven't like already figured it out is, we made up. Yeah. He made me give him, well, do a sex thing for him, just to show I love him, but it wasn't so bad. Sort of sweet, y'know. I mean, I'm still a virgin, too, more or less, but I get all wet just thinking about how manly he is. And he didn't hit me, y'know, the way he did before. Except he did like twist my arm a little. Sort of a love-twist, I thought."

I definitely don't want to hear any more about Sheba's sex life, and am not eager to continue the conversation.

But Sheba is. "I wouldn't tell these other guys, since they'd only laugh. They're always laughing about Richie. It's because they're probably afraid of him, since he's like got this way about him, this warrior spirit that puts fear into the hearts of his enemies."

"I don't know Richie that well." I am tempted to add the word *fortunately,* but I hold off. "I don't talk with Richie. I sometimes talk with his brother Joseph."

"You actually talk with Joseph, face to face?"

"More like shout at him, front porch to front porch."

Sheba moves her head closer and confides, "Joseph is a loser, y'know. Richie says so. Richie's gonna become Mayor of Balona some day. He says so, and I believe him." Sheba leans back and bobbles her head in agreement with her opinion.

I say to myself, Well, then, Richie will have something in common with his great-grandfather, Mr. Junior Kuhl. I wonder how Mr. Kuhl would feel about that.

Sheba leans even closer, so that I almost have to scoot my chair back in order to avoid the chance of being sprayed on. "I'll show you something," she says, "but you got to promise not to tell anybody."

120

"Well, I don't know...."

"I'll show you anyways. But don't tell. It's what Richie gave me to show he loves me, y'know. He said he was going to give me a prize Siamese cat, but the stubborn thing died on him while he was trying to teach it some tricks.

"So about this present, he said I shouldn't show it to any-body, since it's like supposed to be a surprise. I told him I wouldn't, but you know how us women are about secrets." She sniffs and giggles, and several staff members glance our way, probably wondering about Sheba's sudden high spirits.

Sheba is wearing a white, long-sleeved cotton sweater that she has buttoned up to her neck on this warm mid-day. The other girls and I are in tank tops or loose blouses because of the ambient temperature. "Wanna see?"

"Sure."

"Remember it's a surprise, so you won't tell?"

"You haven't shown it yet." That is a weasely answer.

Sheba pops open her top three buttons and pulls out a tarnished silver heart-shaped locket on a silver chain. The jewelry appears well used.

It looks familiar.

It looks exactly like Mr. Junior Kuhl's missing Daisy locket. "My goodness, does the locket have a picture of a woman inside it?"

"Well, yeah. Looks sort of like me. Sort of blonde. And on the other side there's like a picture of a man, too, with a mustache and his eyes looking acrost at her. Richie said I could put his picture in there. And I could like cut out a picture of myself and stuff it in there, too. We'll be together always that way. He didn't say that last part, but I like figured that's the way he would've said it if he'd thought to say it out loud."

121

My mind races, considering numerous alternatives as to how to handle this situation.

Sheba rubs the locket, frowns. "I got to say, though, when he like drug this out of his pocket and I got a good look at it, and I saw it was old and beat up, I didn't think that much of it as a gift, y'know." She sniffs. "If you don't mind me saying so, I prefer gold myself, not something that looks like a throwaway you get at the Goodwills. I almost, not quite, but almost told him he should give it to his mother."

Now I lean forward and speak in a low voice. "I have to tell you, Sheba. I've seen your locket before. It belongs to old Mr. Junior Kuhl. He was wearing it around his neck. That woman's picture is of his wife Daisy. He told me that the other day. And now he thinks he's misplaced it."

Sheba's lower lip shoots out and her eyebrows meet in the middle. She hisses, "This's *my* locket. Richie says it's genuine silver, and it's mine."

She shoves herself back from the table. "Not my fault if somebody maybe lost it. So don't you go around saying it belongs to some old dead guy." She buttons her sweater, sniffs twice.

"Afraid you're wrong," I say. "It would seem that Richie stole it, or at least borrowed it."

"Don't you dare tell about this, hear? Or I'll tell Richie, and he'll get you. You'll feel his wrath. Don't you dare."

That is the end of our conference, and I go home. Of course, I don't dare *not* tell. First thing I do when I get home is phone Constable Cod Gosling. Unfortunately Cod, who doesn't deign to carry a cellphone, is probably out in front of his office on his bench eating popcorn. Or perhaps he is at Frank's Soupe de Jour—quasi-French, and definitely Balona French—having a couple of

Franksburgers or korndogs. I resolve to get back to him and report what appears to be a crime.

Then I think a bit more. Perhaps Mr. Junior Kuhl had actually given the locket to Richie, and then forgot about making the gift.

It would be unfair and at least awkward if that were the case and I accused Richie of stealing from his great-grandpa.

I decide to bring the matter up with Mr. Junior Kuhl. I put a cold can of soda in my backpack, an offering to Mr. Kuhl's thirst.

11

A sensational murder
may have been committed

Mr. Junior Kuhl is so eager to tell me more about the Great San Francisco Earthquake of 1906 that I am not able to ask the personal question I think might be important to him. Sheba's attitude has really irritated me, so I very much want to quiz Mr. Kuhl about his missing locket, get to the bottom of this mystery. I pop open the soda and pour it into a glass.

"Hey, I never touch that stuff," he growls. "Too sweet." Noticing my spontaneous frown, he adds, "But thanks for the memory." He points to my chair and begins at once, I sipping on the ginger ale.

He's right. It is too sweet.

MR. KUHL: You smell that smoke smell in the air? Even my beat-up old nose can smell that. Must've been a big fire in Balona last night. That smell really takes me back. You ever been real, real hungry? Yeah? Well, I guess most kids feel that way. A minute or two before dinner time. But before me and Poppy got to the soup kitchen on Mission Street back then, I felt I was gonna perish. Both from hunger and thirst and from the huge big smoke smell. A whole lot stronger than right now in Balona. In fact, so strong and sharp back then that, when you took a breath, you could feel a sharp pain right down in the bottom of your lung.

"Oh, I'm so hungry and thirsty I got a pang right here," I told Poppy in kind of a loud voice. I pointed at my belly. And fact is, I hadn't had a bite to eat since the night before. We'd had beet soup and thick-buttered pumpernickel for supper. That fine sweet soup was red as a, well, you could figger out what it was red as. [Mr. Kuhl chuckles.] "And so heavy you could had to chew it. It was one of Mama's specialities. Poppy's favorite.

As for me, I would prefer a nice roasted beef tongue. Or a pan of fried brains. Or a whole fried-up chicken, eats that we didn't often have. But that beet soup did make my mouth water. Just to think about.

Poppy said, "Well, just think about your poor Mama and the little ones back at the cemetery without anything at all to eat. And maybe your hunger pang will quiver down some."

Well, that made me think, all right. But it never toned down that belly pang at all. I was straining my eyeballs for a look at that famous soup kitchen. I thought it was gonna be a building with a huge big kettle. Like the pots that cannibals use, over a fire.

And a lot of people bending over it with cups and big spoons. Drinking soup, y'know? But we could hear more explosions down past the train station. And over toward the docks. So we figured the fire wasn't anywheres near put out yet. We hurried on. I looked up at Poppy while we hastened on our way. Tears was dripping off of his fine big mustache. Down his chin.

"How come you're crying, Poppy?"

"I just can't stop. We lost our babies, boy. My fault, since I didn't do a goldarn thing to get to 'em. That's why." You probably notice my Poppy never cussed real cuss words. Not even after we settled here in Balona where even the women are champion cussers. He always strived to be a gentleman. Even with his hairy belly showing and his sleeves cut short. Said he learnt the way of the gentleman from a Japanese warrior he once knew up at Gold Hill.

I tried to make him feel better. "The house fell down, Poppy. Not your fault. Nobody's fault. There wasn't no way to get to those babies. And the fire was too big."

Poppy's head drooped down. "No, I should've gone back in there right away. It would've been the right thing to do." He made a big sigh. "Besides, your dear mother will never forgive me."

And, fact is, I don't think she ever did. But it got me thinking. Probably if I hadn't just stood there and watched the babies burn, if I'd went back in there, I'd have saved 'em. It was the right thing to do. So it was my fault, too.

TERY: But you'd have been dead, too. And it was nobody's fault. You said so yourself.

MR. KUHL: I'd maybe be dead, but I'd be a hero. And Mama would've finally loved me. After the fire, Poppy still loved me. But Mama, she never loved me then at all. But I strived on, got rich, became a leader. Daisy said she loved me. Said so a couple times. Early on, anyways.

TERY: You said your father was a hero, and that he had some hero money.

MR. KUHL: Well, that was later, not quite yet. Right then we was going to get something to eat. And there it was. There was that famous soup kitchen. I knew it was, because that's exactly what Poppy said it was. "There's the soup kitchen, Junior. Now we can maybe get us a bite to eat and swage our thirst."

I didn't see the big cannibal kettle at all. There was just a hasty set-up of a bunch of part-burnt doors that somebody had nailed flat on top of a few two-by-fours. To make a long table. And there was a huge crowd of people. Grabbing sangwidges and eggs off of that table. No soup that you could see.

Nothing to drink.

My tongue practically shriveled.

"Clear back," hollered this big guy holding a handful of greenbacks, and people cleared back. But everybody kept trying to get a closer look at the food on the table. I was working up a real mouthful of spit. Anticipating that meal. "Get back in line, and everybody will get something. Keep on crowding in like that, and we'll pack up and go somewheres else where people got some manners."

So we got into line. It didn't take too long. By the time we got up to the front of the line my jaws was dripping like a dog with hydrophobia.

The sangwidges was yellow cheese slices and sweet-looking pink ham on hunks of actual thick white bread. Looked delectitious to the extreme. The eggs was hard-boiled and looked tasty, too. Only there wasn't any savor salt to dip 'em in. And they would make you thirsty. And there was nary a drop to wet your whistle with. I was hungry, all right, but I was even thirstier.

"Ten dollars for a sangwidge and a fiver for a egg," said the man with the greenbacks. "Pay up or move aside." A couple hard-looking fellers stood next to him, giving all of us the eagle eye. Poppy spoke up.

"We thought this was a charity, for burnt-out folk."

"You thought wrong, Dude," said the feller, snickering at Poppy's hairy belly. "This's a business enterprise. You want charity, go to church." The hard-looking fellers laughed. Men behind us pushed us out of the way. Gave over their cash. Grabbed their sangwidges and eggs.

"What're we gonna do for food and drink, Poppy?"

"We're gonna suck in our gut and strive on, boy." He leant down and picked up a pebble off of the street, rubbed it off with his thumb, handed it to me. "You just put this under your tongue, Junior. It'll take off the biggest thirst until we find us some charity. You can do it, I know. What worries me now is how your mama is carrying on."

So we strived on without food or drink. Like most of the people on the street. Except for the gangs still looting the bars. And wetting their whistles with ill-gotten booze. In those days San Francisco had a lot more bars than it has today. Even today it's got a lot. I'm told.

The army wasn't around Mission and Third yet. They was mostly blowing up buildings, I guess. To keep the fire away. So the liquor looters had theirselfs a good old time. By this time they was not only looting and whistle-wetting, but singing right next to the smoke and fire. One ratty-looking feller was dancing a jig, with the others clapping him on.

My Poppy said we needed to get back to Mama "before she does something stupid." Poppy never said such a thing where Mama could hear him say it. But when we was alone, he would confide such confidential manly things to his oldest son that way. I learnt to treat my own wife like I loved her dearly and always took good care of her. I learnt that way from Poppy, and always did it. Even though Daisy sometimes accused me of having opinions.

TERY: [I notice that, as he speaks these words, Mr. Kuhl feels around his chest and neck, as if he is searching for his locket. I think that this is not the time to interrupt his tale, so I don't ask about the locket.]

MR. KUHL: So then, walking all this time, we went up Mission Street for a while. Then crossed back over to Market. Fires seemed to be breaking out everywhere.

TERY: You describe your Poppy's coat as his "derringer coat." Is that a brand name, like a Burberry?

MR. KUHL: No, his derringer coat was where he kept his derringer, of course. You couldn't leave a thing like that laying around where there was kids in the house. So he'd always leave it in a special pocket. Hung up on a peg on the wall, and inside of his coat.

I had been sore tempted a few times to peek in there when I saw that coat hanging on its peg. But Poppy said he'd whup me if I even touched it. So I never did. Not then, anyways.

Y'know, it's a real fierce temptation for any kid, a young man especially, to have a famous gun — that's what a derringer is, in case you didn't know — right there where it's practically in your very own hand.

TERY: A derringer is a gun.

MR. KUHL: A derringer is a small pistol. Pretty small. Not like your six-shooter or your long-barrel policeman's pistol. Or your big, heavy cal'vry sidearm. It's actually, well, sort of a gambling man's gun. Fits right there in the palm of your hand. For emergencies, y'know. But it makes a great loud noise. Powerful, to boot. Most fellers can't hit the side of a barn even with a big pistol. But Poppy was a crack shot with that tiny little double-barrel derringer.

130

It happens that I took after him in that talent. And my grandson Kenworth is a fine shot, too, y'know.

TERY: Your Poppy carried that little gun around with him all the time?

MR. KUHL: No law against it. Not like nowadays. Those were dangerous times, and Poppy was in a dangerous profession. Sure, he carried it. I'm getting to that.

So there we went, marching up Market Street keeping to the north side of the street. People still passing us by. But going down the other way, towards the Ferry Building. But that ferryboat crowd was pretty much thinned out, since it was still pretty early. I guess the word was getting around about the boat supposably loading up later at ten-thirty.

TERY: I wonder how the word got around, since you didn't have TV back in those days.

MR. KUHL: You're right about that. And no radio, even. But there was those yellow printed posters got nailed up right away, all over on the electric poles, telling folks the latest news and rules, eksedra.

Anyways, up ahead, on the south side of the street the fire was getting pretty fierce. At one building especially, a crowd was standing back from the heat. Looking and pointing. No fire engine was there. No army either.

"He's trapped under there," one feller shouted, pointing at the flaming building. And there you could see this yellow-headed man in a black coat. Alive all right, but with a huge big beam smack dab across his middle, pinning him down.

And all around his legs was fire, it being fed by heaps of broken wood. And walls. And furniture. And cloth. Flames creeping up on him fast.

He was thrashing his arms about. Hollering, "Get me out of here, somebody, for God's sake. I'm burning up."

Nobody was moving a lick, since there wasn't nobody who could get close enough because of that hot fire. Even if you could get close enough, ten men together couldn't lift that huge big beam off of the poor feller.

We would have to watch him roast like a Hawaii barbecue right there in front of us.

The poor trapped feller started screaming along with his thrashing. And then he stopped it for a second and hollered out, clear as a bell, "Somebody kill me. Please, God, kill me."

And Poppy made a groaning sound and coughed in a big breath, like he was crying again. "Dear Lord," went Poppy, "I cannot let this be my fault, too." He turned to me. "Give me the bandana, Junior."

I took my bandana off where it had slipped down to my neck. Poppy grabbed it in his hand. "Turn away from this, boy," he said, pulled his hat down tight and marched across the street straight into the smoke and flames. I tried to stop him.

Clutched at the tail of his coat. He was already gone.

All I could do was scream. I couldn't stop myself. People around me screamed, too, to see Poppy do that.

We all could see and hear what Poppy did when he got up to where the man was thrashing about and shrieking, pants legs already flaming. Poppy stuck his bandana out toward the man.

"Put it over your eyes, sir," Poppy hollered, since by then the flames were making quite a to-do. And so the man did.

And Poppy reached in his coat.

Took out his derringer.

Shot the poor suffering man straight through the head.

Then he staggered backwards out of the flames.

132

Poppy's eyebrows was all gone. And his eyelashes, as was most of his fine big mustache. And all his hat in front. His clothes was steaming and smoking. Poppy kept blinking his eyes, which I guess anybody would do who'd been that close to such a fire. He stood there leaning over, his hands on his knees, gagging and heaving breaths, puke and spit streaming out of his mouth and nose onto the pavement stones.

Nobody in the crowd said a word, until one real tall man in a brown suit and bowler hat and yellow shoes and a necktie with a tie pin said in a choked-up voice, "That was the bravest, most decent thing I ever seen." And the people started to clap their hands. Even while you could see the man in grave peril who had now cashed in his chips, of course, catch fire. Which sight I won't describe, since it is not describable. Since besides, I still see it whenever I close my eyes.

"We seen it, too," went a couple of firemen who had just arrived, probably wondering what they could do.

The yellow-shoes man said to Poppy, "Please come with me, sir. I want my boss, Mayor Schmitz, to meet you. He should be at his emergency headquarters, only a block or so away from here. Please come with me. Please."

Poppy was out of it. Awake, but not exactly, if you feature what I'm saying. He looked a sight, what with a wet-looking red face. His hat brim and front hair and great mustache and shaggy eyebrows all gone. His coat sleeves short. And his belly showing, not so hairy any more.

So me and Poppy went after the tall man. We was followed by the two firemen and most of the crowd who didn't care to stand witness to the roasting of the corpse. They all probably wanted to get a closer look at Mayor Schmitz. Find out whether the mayor was going to throw Poppy in

San Quentin Prison for murder. Maybe the mayor would turn him over to the army for the firing squad. All those people had seen Poppy shoot the burning man in the head. Commit murder.

I was wondering, too, after Poppy got firing-squadded or sent to San Quentin for life, who was going to take care of me. And Mama and the little ones.

And Grover, too, of course.

~

Mr. Junior Kuhl is shedding tears as he finishes this hyper-graphic vision of his father rushing into the fire. Mr. Kuhl has placed his hand over his eyes. He turns his head slowly from side to side. I am eager to know what had happened next in his tale, but the devastated appearance of this sad old man suggests to me that I should now leave him to his reminiscences. It seems to me that this must have been, after all, not a tall tale told at Ned's Sportsbar, but the recounting of a real experience.

As I rise to leave, I reach over and pat him on the shoulder, hoping that my touch might console him a bit. Instead, he breaks into sobs, muttering, "Oh, Poppy, Poppy."

And that finishes the interview for the day.

12

Balona elder statesman reveals dissatisfaction with diet

Mr. Junior Kuhl's riveting description of his quake experiences gets me to wondering about earthquakes in general.

I e-mail my brother Jack:

Did we ever have an earthquake in Balona?

Jack responds in his new e-mail style:

sure. a few yrs ago, when sf had their last big 1, we cd feel it here. dont u (of all peple) rember? acty, we have ltle 1s evry 1s in a wile.

Of course, I (of all peple) remember, but the memory isn't completely sensory, and I have been thinking about big earthquakes and recall no such phenomenon.

About the last big one, I was at home. It was about five o'clock in the afternoon, and it seemed as if a high wind had suddenly, briefly caught us. The house creaked several times, and on the living room wall my daddy's big color photo of Mommy was jarred off-center. Of course, I was a lot younger then and occupied at the time with an art project, concerned only that water from my watercolor bowl had spilled onto the table. I hadn't paid all that much attention to the experience until Daddy came home, and then we all had watched results of the Bay Area disaster on TV. It was indeed terrible.

Jack adds:

> n we cd have nother gd 1,2, sins were on r own fault line here in blona. the blona fault is a minor crack in the erth, but a fault nevertheless. r levee cd brk and we cd be under water agn, this time bigtime. ive got to get back to anatomy. wrk on ur schubert.

Jack uses the word "again" because only a couple of years ago much of Balona was for a while under four feet of water resulting from a break in the levee that usually keeps the Yulumne River from wetting our knees.

Having left Mr. Junior Kuhl this day, I organize my notes and think about what I have been hearing in Mr. Kuhl's voice. Chiefly ringing there is the respect for Julius C. Kuhl, Senior, a great man in Junior's mind — kind, considerate, loving, but perhaps not particularly practical. I should write my account to make sure readers understand and appreciate the more affirmative characteristics. I also wonder what there was about twelve-year-old Junior Kuhl that caused his daddy to find Junior so lovable.

Of course, I must keep in mind that it is no one but Junior who is relating the details of who said what, felt what, et cetera. My feelings about my own daddy are like

Mr. Junior Kuhl's perceptions of Mr. Senior Kuhl. Daddy doesn't have a mustache, though, and doesn't like guns at all. Daddy is tree tall, and has muscles that show in his arms. He has big clean hands with fingernails that he keeps cut short. He has brown hair and brown eyes and white teeth and smooth skin. Women say he looks like a movie star, but he is also shy and self-effacing, always saying that I'm a lot smarter than he is.

I'll reserve comment about that.

Daddy doesn't make much money working for the *Courier*, so I guess some people would describe him as "not practical," but he does get commissions for his sculptures, and creates a lot of those, big and small. I can play the piano and paint a little, but art seems to just flow out from Daddy through his work.

We could get along nicely on Daddy's income without taking any money at all from Claire's inheritance and Penny's own bequest from Pastor Preene, Penny's natural father. But Penny is always buying things for the house and gifts for Daddy, probably out of her own money. She does buy stuff for Jack and me, too. I suppose we as a family must now be considered, in Sheba's terms, filthy rich in Balona.

That could be another reason that kids might think I'm weird—besides Hopalong, the vocabulary, and my red stockings.

My mother was tall and had a dark-blonde bob. Beautiful soft hair that became shorter and thinner, until she had no hair at all, not even eyebrows or eyelashes, and only a bandana around her smooth-skinned head.

I recalled her image vividly as I listened to Mr. Junior Kuhl describe his father's appearance after the incident with the burning man. My mother's loss of hair resulted not from fire, but from her terrible illness. I remember her as good-smelling and clean and pretty. She hugged me a lot and kissed me, demonstrated her affection for me, something my daddy doesn't do.

My mother worked in the bank on Front Street until she got cancer and died. Penny used to come over and read to my sick mother and give her massages when Mommy was drugged but still writhing and groaning in most awful pain.

Penny would hold Mommy's hand and generally act friendly.

I could already read very well at that age, and understood pretty much the vocabulary and the sense of what I was reading. I could have read to my mother.

She liked the lyrics from the Beatles and the rock group Grateful Dead and old poets Tennyson and Browning and Yeats. I liked the sounds that the poets created, too, but Mommy evidently preferred Penny's grown-up voice.

"Go ride your tricycle, Tery, or color or paint. Have some fun. Life is too short for a little girl to be cooped up with an invalid," she would say. Any way you look at it, she would say, life is too short.

She said it to Daddy, too, but he never went out and had fun. He stayed with her until the end. Sometimes he sat on the front porch glider and looked at the sunset. I vaguely remember that the scent of blossoms from our two orange trees was very strong there. Memory plays tricks. Even mine. Maybe the scent was Daddy's aftershave. Jack would sit at Daddy's right, and I at his left. The three of us would just sit, looking, not saying a word.

I remember hearing the car noises from First Avenue, Obahchan playing Chopin, neighbor Mrs. Bapsie Kuhl screaming threats at Joseph, birds twittering, and Daddy's nose making tiny whistling noises. Maybe he had a cold or hay fever. Through the open window we could hear the clacking of the machine that helped Mommy breathe. Once in a while I would reach over and touch Daddy's hand. In the weeks that my mother lay dying, Daddy's aura turned from light blue to indigo.

I wonder if Mr. Junior Kuhl feels that life is too short. He had also mumbled, "When I d-i-e, I'll go to H-e-l, for sure." But that's obviously not something I should ask him about. And I don't know whether or not life is too short. It can be beautiful. It can surely be terribly sad.

I recently suggested as much to Mommy. She said that whether it's too short or too long, too sad or too happy, it all depends on your perspective.

"I don't understand what you mean," I said.

"Well, just keep thinking about your blessings, stop continually doubting yourself, and some day you'll figure it out." Then she faded out of my perception, a habit she has developed lately.

～

It seems to me that I had left Mr. Junior Kuhl in an awfully low mood, so I drop in on him before lunch, to make sure he is all right. For the first time I find him standing. He is at his window, on his toes, leaning on the sill, trying to see over that bush that obscures his clear view of living Balona. He turns as I open his door.

I am surprised to discover that I am taller than he by almost a head.

"Well, come on in and set a spell." He points at my regular chair. "I been exercising my limbs here and there. It's a life-long habit, exercising, but I'm now feeling a bit shaky in the legs and ready to relax." He sits, tugging at his hospital gown and covering his hairless legs with gown and robe. His modest gestures are reminiscent of the way my mother covered her skinny self in the last phases of her illness, trying to look neat and presentable, no matter how miserable she felt.

Reminding myself that I am an optimist, I make my voice cheerful, put on a lip-smile. "I see that you're able to be up and around."

"Sure. See there, I got a walker, keeps me from falling on my butt." Sure enough, there is such a device, a waist-high metal frame with small wheels on the front legs, none on the two rear legs. The walker is folded next to his bed. I had not paid attention to it before.

I ask, "Mr. Kuhl, you say you exercise every day?"

"Kevin comes in. Gets me up and around twice a day. Three times if you don't count lunch, when Kevin makes me ride in a chair. But the lunches around here don't have taste, y'know." Mr. Kuhl makes a face illustrating blah. "I'd better like something good and strong for my taste bugs. Liver and onions, say. Or sauerkraut and weenies. Around here they grind up everything until it's soupy. And they won't salt it worth siccum."

Mr. Kuhl's description of the institutional diet sounds accurate. My mother's diet in her last days was chemical, snaked by tubes into her arm. "Take those things out of me. Let me go," she would say.

Jack is now advising me, too: "Let Mom go," he says. But Mommy is a comfort to me. Losing her, cutting her off, is not possible right now.

It would be like losing love entirely.

"I figure they charge me seventeen-fifty for every lunch," remarks Mr. Kuhl, "even I don't eat it. You know that fat boy?"

Mr. Kuhl's abrupt change of subject reminds me of how Sheba changes the subject in the middle of an idea.

"The huge man who works with Mr. Carbunzle?"

"No, no. I said already. That's Kevin. Kevin's got a whole lot of muscles. I mean the fat boy." Mr. Kuhl pounds on the arm of his chair. "The *fat* boy. Who is that boy?"

"I think probably you're referring to your great-grandson, Richie Kuhl?"

"That's the one. That's the fat boy. Do you know he's a blood relative? Doesn't look like it, though. Takes after his mama, Kenworth says. Kenworth is a good boy." Mr. Kuhl pauses, nods several times. "My boy Lee named Kenworth after a truck. Lee named all his boys after trucks. Something about power, he said. The power part didn't take with Kenworth. But he's my best grandson, brings me a sangwidge. Reads me the paper. Except Kenworth isn't around lately."

Mr. Kuhl frowns. "The fat boy is not a good boy. I may be sorry that he's a blood relative."

"Has your great-grandson disappointed you?" I am trying to be discreet about the possible theft of the locket.

"Y'know, it's not only Daisy what's gone missing. Now I can't find my good old watch either. Had it in my drawer right here just yesterday." Mr. Kuhl sighs. "When you get old as me, you don't look at your watch often as a young whippersnapper does. But I am pretty sure I looked at my fine old timepiece yesterday."

I ask, "Your watch is a wristwatch?"

"Lordy, no. I had one of those contraptions once. When I got a few years on me and began shrinking, that watch started dangling." Mr. Kuhl shows how the wristwatch dangled right off his age-shrunken wrist and onto the floor. "Splat, it went. No wristwatch for me. My watch is

141

the good old gold watch I inherited when Poppy passed over. Got a genuine green leather fob and JCK graven into the genuwine solid 24-karat gold cover. Initials, y'know. Y'wanna help me look for it?" Mr. Kuhl heaves himself about, turning his neck and groaning as he does so. "They got me in the ribs, too, those wraiths did." He pauses, locks his eyes on mine. "D'you think that fat boy is a good boy?"

I hesitate just a moment before I respond. "I think Richie is not a very nice person." Mr. Kuhl thinks a while, then nods slowly, making a bad-taste face.

We search behind his pillows, in drawers and in his closet. I glance under his bed. I peek into his toilet room and see only false teeth on a glass shelf and other stuff that I suppose you'd expect to find there for an old man's convenience. It's possible that the watch is stashed under his mattress. We don't search there.

"Well," Mr. Kuhl says, "might as well sit down there, and let's get on with it."

13

Hero proclaimed and rewarded in surprise move

MR. KUHL: Where the San Francisco City Hall fell down, all that was left was this gold-colored upside-down cup sitting up there atop some iron work. I'm talking a huge big cup, like for a giant to turn over and drink out of. Stacks of smoking junk all around it. That beautiful new building was trashed for sure.

It at least wasn't burnt up.

But Mayor Schmitz needed to find a place to headquarter himself and all his friends and assistants. The plaza across the street was full of dead bodies being laid out in rows. Most of them covered up, but not all. More being hauled in all the time. Probably enough to fill up the whole space.

TERY: [Mr. Kuhl looks down at his hands, folded in his lap. He moves his head from side to side.]

MR. KUHL: You probably seen bodies on the TV. Maybe even a bunch of 'em laid out in some kind of a big tragedy? A fire or flood? Bodies sprawled out everywhere? Yes?

But seeing real dead bodies laid out is different. Made me hurt down in my gut."

[Mr. Kuhl nods to himself.] "You see it on the TV all the time. Dead bodies. Real thing's not like a TV show at all. Not at all. Maybe I already said that."

TERY: [We sit for a full minute in silence. I am disciplining myself, not pushing.]

MR. KUHL: Actually, the day was getting to be pretty nice. If you didn't think about the flames climbing up the block and all the dead people around the corner laid out in the plaza. And the broke-down buildings everywhere. And did I say about the wild horses and the crazy automobile drivers in the streets?

And the beat-up-looking almost-dressed people running around, wandering, staggering? This was in San Francisco, our beautiful City by the Bay. And not a sangwidge in sight. Speaking of same, did somebody bring me a sangwidge today?

TERY: I'm sorry. I'll remember next time I come.

MR. KUHL: Well, it's because I have this empty feeling from remembering all this. [Mr.Kuhl massages his abdomen.] Anyways, where was I?

TERY: You were with your father going up to the mayor's tent, his emergency headquarters, you said.

MR. KUHL: Yes, we soon learned that the mayor had went around into Market Street. Had his office people set up shop in a dirt-colored tent on the corner where there was a sandy lot all ready for a new building.

TERY: Were the fires still burning?

MR. KUHL: Well, sir, the fire in that area was just getting started. Hadn't come as far as Mayor Schmitt's new place. That headquarters was like a big company office there, held down by ropes and sandbags — sand, rocks, and, naturally, a few bits of horse pucky for the office floor. And it was much exposed to the smoke and fog and the elements. Canvas sides flapping in the spanking breeze that was also rustling up the pieces of paper in the boxes they'd managed to pull out of the fell-down city hall.

This mayor's office was a temporary space, so it could be picked up and moved in haste, y'know, coal oil lamps and all. Even to the little printing press way in the back of the tent, clanking up and down, back and forth. Caught my eye first. A man with sleeve garters and a green visor turning out yellow flyers. Official documents, of course. Telling people what to do.

I did that, too, when I was Balona mayor. Only people paid no attention at all to my flyers. Just like Daisy.

TERY: [Mr. Kuhl closes his eyes and is again silent. In the time he spends contemplating, I recite silently two entire verses of a Schubert lyric.]

MR. KUHL: But that emergency office was a busy place, let me tell you. We followed the big man with the yellow shoes right inside that tent. Up to where a person with a huge wide butt — sorry — was bending over a table. It was the mayor. He was pointing at something. Talking to an army soldier. The yellow-shoes man leaned over. Said some words into Mayor Schmitz's ear.

The mayor and the soldier both turned right around to look at us.

The soldier had a dangle of gold strings bunched up on each shoulder of his blue uniform. A row of bright-colored medals pinned on his coat. Maybe he was a general.

Mayor Schmitz was a tall man, too, like the general. Except he had a huge big belly, sideburn whiskers as well as a chin-beard and mustache. Seemed to be covered in gold jewelry. Chains dangling from his vest. Purple gem sparkling from his necktie knot. Red ones along his vest front. I guess he'd had plenty of time to get dressed. Or maybe he'd been up all night, on official business. Mayors do that, y'know—stay up all night, officialing.

Well, as the yellow-shoes man told him about Poppy's murderous deed, Mayor Schmitz's eyes got huge big. The general pulled on his own mustache. Looked serious.

"I tried to hold back, your Honor," went Poppy, gasping and coughing a bit, "but I had to help that man in his hour of need." Most of the women who had followed us, and even a few of the men, had tears streaking the smoke stains on their faces. "That's right. He did right," they were saying through their stains. You couldn't tell if Poppy was crying or not, since his cheeks, red as a beet, seemed all wet. From his burns.

By this time, there wasn't nobody in the mayor's tent who wasn't paying attention to me and Poppy. I pulled myself up. Stood straight as a beanpole. The way Poppy taught me. Maybe fifty people gathered to hear if there was a scandal to be told and, if so, who was going to hang.

Poppy was standing there now, looking at the rocks on the ground. Mayor Schmitz and the general and everybody else was looking at Poppy, including me. I was wondering when they would haul Poppy off to jail, and what would I do then. But the mayor calmed down my fears. "Sir," he said to Poppy. "These people say that what you did was not only brave, but also extraordinarily humane. And I must agree. So instead of incarcerating you, I intend to cite you for heroism."

Then he turned to a feller with glasses pinched onto his nose and told him to work up a certificate for Poppy.

Whereupon the general also spoke right up in a loud voice. "And I intend to cite you for gallantry," which I later figured out was sort of the same thing as heroism. The general then felt over his own chest. Looked down at his row of ribbons. He put his hand under a shiny gold medal hanging on the end of a long red ribbon. "Sir," he said to Poppy, "what you did in a flaming minute is far more heroic than anything I ever did in an entire campaign. Please accept this in token of my regard." And the general lifted the medal off of his chest. Reached it across. Pinned it on Poppy's derringer coat lapel.

Poppy looked like he'd been hit on the head with a brick. His eyes sort of rolled back in his head. I thought he was going to fall to the ground. But the man with the yellow shoes held him up by one elbow. I was standing at the other side, ready to do my part, too. Everybody clapped, including me. I have that fine medal to this day, tucked away in a safe place. I hope safe.

TERY: You have the medal in the bank, I guess.

MR. KUHL: No, I got it right here somewheres. Maybe in the drawer there.

TERY: And you still have the certificate.

MR. KUHL: Never did get that one. Must've got lost in the shuffle, when they had other things to do back then. They had to move headquarters several times, to stay out of harm's way. Poppy never worried about it. Mama used to rag on him about it, since she wasn't there to see the deed and the ceremony. I told her all about the medal, too, but maybe she never did believe us. Women sometimes don't believe their husbands' hero stories. Or what their kids tell them, y'know. Poppy put the medal away in his pocket, but Mama believed the money when she saw it, all right.

TERY: Money, you say.

MR. KUHL: That's what I just said. M-o-n-e-y, what makes the world go around. Well, sir, back in the tent the mayor had picked up a box and put a bill in it. A ten-spot, I think maybe it was. "Let's send this good man on his way with something else to remember us by," he said, and passed the box on among the assembled multitudes.

Now, sometimes when this happens in a group, and everybody sees the box or the hat or the collection plate coming in their direction, they sort of melt away. Not this time. I watched.

Everybody who had a pocket to pull money out of put something in that box. When it came back, Mayor Schmitz handed it to Poppy. "With our best wishes for a full recovery, sir, and please do wish the same to our sad and formerly lovely city."

Poppy bowed not only his head, but his entire body from the waist. Like he was bowing to a king. But of course he grabbed a holt into the box. No jingle to it at all. Just bills. Poppy didn't count it out right then. He later explained that it wouldn't have been polite to count it out in front of everybody. Specially when people standing there had on barely enough clothes on to cover theirselfs.

But the bills in his hand made a wad big enough to choke a horse.

"Don't spend it all in one place," said a sharp-looking dude in a flat black hat and a bright green vest. His eyes was glued on Poppy's cash-full fist. Kept licking his lips.

The man in the yellow shoes spoke into Poppy's ear, "Put that money away, sir. These are hard times, and there are desperate men about."

148

Poppy stuffed the bills in his derringer coat pocket. Patted it flat, but the pocket still bulged out with all that nice cash. The feller in the green vest looked the other way. Sort of whistled to himself.

"Let's see if we can find us some food, Junior." So me and Poppy eked our way back towards the cemetery. Expecting and hoping to find Mama and the little ones safe and sound. And Grover, too, of course.

On the way back up Van Ness there was already fire on one side of that street in a lot of places. The fire was still growing. The firemen were moving a lot slower, all tired out, but still trying to put out the flames. It sure looked like a useless task what with no water in the mains. And the breeze whipping up the blazes.

Then we saw a crowd starting to gather at an army flatbed wagon stopped on the side of the street up a ways where there was no fire. We could see soldiers all around it. Soldiers up on the box, driving the team. And all the soldiers had rifles with bayonets. And behind the army wagon was a fire department wagon.

We hurried our steps to see what we could see. Figuring maybe up ahead there was something to eat and drink.

Sure enough, the firemen—not my firemen, but good enough—were pumping out water into what containers people had brought. There was a hose screwed onto the side of the engine. Small enough hose to drink out of. The poor wore-out fire horses looked like they could use a drink. More people were coming every minute.

Then we saw a really happy sight.

A soldier threw aside a tarpaulin, a canvas cover over the bed of the wagon. And there from underneath that tarp appeared a huge big stack of bread loafs. The people cheered. The soldiers threw a loaf to every pair of hands stretched out for one. Me and Poppy had two pairs of hands, so we got two loafs.

"We got this stack here from the bakery up on Eddy Street," hollered a soldier. "A mob was just about to loot all, so we lined up, scared 'em off, and took over. This other stack here, bread and rolls and cans of meat, is from a grocery up Van Ness a ways, where the owner was trying to charge poor honest people ten dollars a loaf. We liberated the whole kaboodle. That feller is still hollering, I bet. No charge for these at all," he added, which was nice, since a lot of the crowd turned their pockets out. To show they didn't have any money.

I had been concerned that Poppy might start giving our Hero Cash away to poor people, orphans, and the homeless. Something he was ordinarily inclined to do when he'd had a few beers. Or when he'd just won a pot and Mama wasn't around. There was certainly a lot of homeless around. But I guess he wasn't thinking normally. Did not do that noble deed. And we kept our wad of hero bills, along with two loafs and a couple cans of meat. Right off, I wondered how we was going to open up those cans with our can opener hid under many tons of rubble.

Then I remembered Poppy's good old knife. He kept it strapped under his pantsleg, down near his ankle. "For emergencies," he would say. I was so hungry. I suggested we sit down and open up one of them cans and make us some tasty sangwidges. "Nope," said Poppy, "we'll wait till we get to Mama and the little ones."

"And Grover," I said to Poppy, reminding him. I always took good care of Grover. Even though Grover turned out to be a Balona rat. But never mind.

"Sure. Grover, too," Poppy said.

So I got to thinking some useful thoughts.

It would be useful, I thought if I put our stuff into my suitcase right away. Then I could go back in line and get another loaf, this one for Mama. Poppy said he thought that would not be a good idea. "What if everybody did that?" he said. And that got me to thinking nobler thoughts.

While we got our fill of water, drinking direct out of the hose, I noticed the dude in the green vest standing nearby. Looking very hard like he wasn't watching Poppy. He was pulling on his hat brim and looking every which way but in our direction. It was pretty obvious that he actually was looking at Poppy. I decided not to mention that fact since Poppy was still gasping some. I figured I could be wrong about Green-Vest.

Anyways, we finally did put our goods into my suitcase for me to carry. Poppy wasn't feeling too good. Staggering some. Poppy turned his hat around so he had a piece of a hat brim in front, sort of like a baseball cap. Sheltered his face and eyes. Also didn't look so funny. So it was me who carried that heavy suitcase. All the way back home.

I should say, all the way back to the cemetery. I spied behind us from time to time, looking sideways so as not to be obvious about it. I noticed Green-Vest still there. Quite a ways back. But I figured maybe, since he hadn't tried to do anything, maybe he was a Pinkerton. Maybe he was just a nice helpful detective, watching over us.

Finally we reached the cemetery. What we found there surprised us considerable. But I'm running out of steam right now. Need to take forty winks, y'know. You also hear me gurgling down here? In honor of my hunger. That's the kind of thing you got to consider whether you can put off satisfying it.

Or if a nap is a better idear.

Mr. Kuhl nods off, and I decide I should let him recuperate. As I leave, I encounter Mr. Carbunzle, this time looking the other way, seeming to be trying to avoid me.

I have long legs and catch up with him, tap him on the back of his elbow.

"Well. I just didn't expect you again already, Miss." He smiles with his lips. "You are a member of the Alexander Ordway family, are you not?"

I nod. "I'm his granddaughter."

"Well, I am always at your service, Miss." If Mr. Carbunzle had a broad-brimmed hat trimmed with feathers, I'm sure he would sweep it off in a flourish. It's nice to be a known relative of somebody like Grandpa.

"Mr. Carbunzle, I notice that Mr. Junior Kuhl has somehow developed a black eye, and he's also complaining of sore ribs, says he was attacked."

"Oh, yes. He frequently tells us tales just like that. When our oldsters fall down, especially our old men, they just seem to need to make some excuse, just defend their manhood, as it were."

"He mentioned that some of his property is missing."

"Oh, ha ha. Well." Mr. Carbunzle frowns.

Mr. Carbunzle stops rubbing his hands, clasps them behind his back, blows out his cheeks, almost in my face, with a *fhoooo*. "Well, that's just another one of those many complaints you have to get used to when you serve our older citizens. If you'll just excuse me now, it's just about lunch time and I have some important duties to see to." Again rubbing his hands, Mr. Carbunzle backs away, turns, and races out of sight.

I shall come back after lunch and offer Mr. Junior Kuhl something to nourish his narration.

152

14

Pioneer's descendant sought for questioning

Just as I turned into the walkway at our house, the sheriff's patrol car screeched to a stop on the corner outside Richie's house. Out of the car stepped two huge men who are Balona natives, friends of my daddy whom I know socially. I say socially, not that we are personal friends, but meaning that I don't know them professionally, not yet having been accused of any crime. The deputies recognized me, waved, went about their business.

Sheriff's Sergeants Paul Hernandez and Warren Wong loped up the Kuhl steps and knocked on the screen door. They are both about six-feet-four and each probably weighs a neatly packaged ton or more, but they move smoothly. Being sports-inclined myself, I would say that they move like athletes.

The deputies waited.

I stood on my own steps, waiting to monitor an interesting event, but nothing happened for a while. We all waited.

The deputies knocked on the door again, and evidently it was Richie's elder brother who came to the door, for Sergeant Hernandez said, "Hello, Joe. Richie home?"

At that point Penny called to me with the news that my lunch was on the table. I don't like to inconvenience anyone, so I went into the house, hoping to finish my meal quickly and return to find out what was happening.

I can hardly slurp up my microwaved *ramen* lunch fast enough. Surely something is happening next door on the Kenworth Kuhl porch that I do not want to miss. I can listen in and learn, if not first-hand, then second-hand about how the law works in Chaud County—all in the interest of good journalism, of course.

It takes me less than five minutes to dispose of my noodles and thank Penny for her microwaving thoughtfulness. In that time Joseph Kuhl has joined the deputies on the Kuhl front porch where they are having a conference, the two officers sitting on the Kuhl glider, moving back and forth, as gliders are inclined to do. Joseph is leaning against the porch banister.

Whereas Richie is short and obese, Joseph is tall and slim. Joseph has very light blond hair and those Vulcan-type ears that many Kuhls have—Mr. Junior Kuhl comes to mind.

Richie squeaks when he talks. Joseph has a rather nice light baritone, but with Balona pronunciation peculiarities, saying dit'n instead of didn't, for example, eksedra for et cetera, wut'n for wouldn't, and ast for ask. I try to avoid these localisms, which I suppose is yet another reason for occasionally being referred to as weird.

During church services and at funerals, not to speak of on the street, Balona men tend to speak to one another

154

almost as loudly as Balona women, so I have little difficulty in hearing the conference across the lawn. I sit on our glider with my notebook in hand, gliding, listening, also observing the active auras of the conferees.

"When did you see him last, Joe?" asks Sergeant Paul.

"Uh. Maybe a week or so," replies Joe. "Or a couple days. He sort of slips in and out. He doesn't like me to keep tabs on him. 'You're not the boss of me. You can't tell me what to do,' is what he's always saying. So where was he last night? I don't know."

The gliding stops. "We didn't ask about last night, Joe," says Sergeant Warren. "Why'd you mention last night?"

"Well, uh, I thought you asked if I seen him last night."

"Where were you last night, Joe?" Sergeant Paul again. The deputies are alternating asking their questions, maybe playing good cop-bad cop. We young people have been taught the technique while watching TV.

Joe says, "I wasn't at the fire. I was right here at home, looking at TV. Or maybe I was up at my office on Front Street, working at my computer, trying to solve a crime."

The gliding begins again.

"What crime is that, Joe?" Sergeant Warren asking.

"Any crime. I got to start solving crimes or nobody is going to hire my private-eye services." When he's not attending classes at Chaud County Community College over in Delta City, Joseph is often at his desk in the Front Street real estate office of Kenworth Kuhl where Joseph's name has been added in large gold letters on the front window.

"You just mentioned the fire, Joe, so you did hear the sirens last night."

"I didn't have nothing to do with that fire. I don't set fires. You need to see somebody else about that."

"Like who, Joe?" Warren's voice is soft.

"Well, I could probably name a few names, like Junior Trilbend or Bobby R. Langsam or Acey Reckenwitt, guys known to like fires, but then I'd get sued, y'know, since I don't actually know."

The lawman leans forward. "You're suggesting that somebody set that fire? It wasn't an electrical short or a gas leak caused it? It wasn't an accident?"

"Oh. Well. I don't know. It probably doesn't make any difference. The fire brigade takes so long to get around to a fire, there's never anything left of a building to get a clue out of it about the evil-doer."

"Evil-doer?" Paul's is speaking up now, "So you do believe last night's fire was arson."

"Well, I figure that might be one reason you're looking for Richie. Richie's got a history."

"Sure has." Sergeant Paul says nothing for a moment. The silence hangs in the warm air. I hear bees, a small plane overhead, Joseph's back yard goat bleating over my left shoulder, my Obahchan playing from the *Goldberg Variations* next door over my right shoulder. "So, you're adult age now, Joe. I guess you're in charge of Richie while your dad's in the hospital and your mom's in jail."

"I guess if anybody's in charge of Richie right now, it'd be me, if I was in charge. But like I said, I don't know where he is, which is a true fact. And, y'know, Cod's been looking for him, too." Cod is Balona's constable, friendly, weighs probably more than our refrigerator, not very active.

"Yeah, we already checked with Cod. So, Joe, I guess you wouldn't mind if we look around Richie's room?"

"Oh. Oh. I mean, you guys and me are fellow pros, I know, and professional courtesy and so on, but, well, no, I don't think." Joseph sits on the top step. "I mean, Richie's

156

my brother. I mean, I don't like him much. I mean, he's a pain in the butt. But he's my brother. Besides, Richie would get even. I would feel his wrath."

"You would feel his wrath?" The two big lawmen laugh. "Where'd you ever hear that?"

"Richie says it all the time. He comes in my room in the middle of the night when I'm sleeping. Stands there and looks at me. Doesn't say a word. Gives me the creeps. But anyways, no, you can't go up there and look around. I got stuff in there myself that you could put me away for."

"How's that, Joe?"

"Well, I was just mentioning." Joe coughs. "Not a fact, y'know. Just like a theoretical possibility."

Motorcycle sounds intrude. The machine with two riders barely enters the block, skids almost to a stop, whirls about, and takes off on First Avenue toward Front Street. The passenger is red-haired Pee Weiner, Sheba's little brother. The driver is Richie Kuhl.

"So, there he is." Joe rises but does not have to point out his observation to the deputies. They are already on their way down the stairs and to their car.

"We'll maybe get back to you, Joe," says Sergeant Warren. I don't hear Joseph's response as the car makes a U-turn and proceeds towards Front Street, rather slowly for officers in pursuit. But it's likely that the sergeants are simply observing, not chasing. I have a feeling they will catch Richie one way or another, as that is the usual scenario.

I decide to speak to Joseph to possibly benefit his great-grandfather. Joseph is still standing on his porch, looking down at the steps, apparently lost in thought. I speak up. "Hi, Joseph. How's things?" This is the standard Balona greeting and requires only a mimetic response.

"Yeah, how's things?"

"Say, did you notice Richie's new watch?"

"I haven't saw Richie lately." Joseph speaks softly.

"I understood that Richie might possibly have a new watch, actually a gold pocket watch with a green fob."

"With a what?"

"It's the little leather strap attached to the top of the watch. You use it to pull the watch from your vest pocket."

"Richie don't wear a vest." This interrogation is getting nowhere. I am too direct to make a good detective.

"Well, see you later."

"Yeah." Joseph retreats into his house. I sit on the porch for a few minutes more and soon hear what everyone on our street knows is one of Joseph's favorite recordings blasting from his upstairs bedroom window: The conclusion of Tchaikovsky's "1812 Overture," the part that features a lot of cannon fire. Joseph is known to play this selection, his window wide open so that all us neighbors can enjoy the musical treat, after each of his major weekly arguments with his mother. I return to the kitchen to prepare a revivifying snack for Mr. Junior Kuhl.

~

Mr. Kuhl is awake and alert. He evidently has taken advantage of one of his seventeen-dollar lunches, for on the front of his robe he has a large dark spot decorated with orange-colored bits, probably carrot. But he quickly unwraps the sandwich I offer him, gums into it at once. "Hey, now, all right."

"You said you like something with a good strong taste, so it's sardines and mayonnaise. I left out the celery and lettuce and sliced off the crusts to make it easier to chew."

158

"Yeah, plenty of mayrnaze, I can tell, mmmm."

I comment, "Your eye looks much improved."

"Lucky I don't need glasses yet. Except everything's getting sort of dimmer. As time goes by, y'know."

I only now realize that in all our contacts, Mr. Kuhl has never worn spectacles. I considered in passing that probably he was unable to read because of his great age. It had not occurred to me that a person a hundred-five-plus years old would not require glasses at all.

But here he is, his pale blue, red-rimmed eyes shining, smooth cheeks crammed full of sandwich, defying age. He says softly, "I don't want to open up my emergency stash. You got something to wash this down with?"

In fact, I have brought a small plastic container of milk. I pour the milk into the empty glass on his bedside table.

"Oh, I been thirsty all my life, but I don't drink that stuff." He shudders. "You drink it if you like it, but I'll tell you something about milk. It's got hormones in it makes you sweat. I like better a Hires. Or you got no rootbeer, then a nice light wine. Or if...well, never mind."

I find a clean glass in Mr. Kuhl's bathroom, fill it with Balona water from the washbowl tap, bring it to him. I drink the milk, not being a milk-drinker, but not willing to waste a perfectly good beverage.

He is drooling a bit. I hand him a tissue, and he wipes his mouth.

"You're taking good care of me, girl. I wisht I had knew you when I was younger. I think I already said that." He seems to be continuing to taste his sardine sandwich, smacking his lips and nodding and smiling. He stops his movements and looks at me. "You're so quiet. You don't smile much. You don't look real happy. I think maybe you got an old soul in a young body. Ever think about that?"

"Never thought about that, Mr. Kuhl. But I'm an optimist, so I don't need to laugh and grin all the time." I tap my chest. "It's here inside."

"Yeah. That's where it's got to be. So, did I tell you about the thirst problem we had back in the San Francisco troubles? I didn't get to that part yet? You got to be an optimist to weather that kind of problem. So, open up your notebook there, and let me give you chapter and verse on some of our excitements."

15

Heroic pioneer reveals more hazards facing family

MR. JUNIOR KUHL: I mentioned that dude with the green vest already. He plays a part in the drama-show I got going here, y'know. You remember that one?

TERY: I remember. He had a flat black hat, too, and licked his lips a lot. The way you describe him, he was a sinister-looking fellow.

MR. KUHL: That's the ticket. And he also had a real sneaky look about him. He kept on following us at a distance. Me carrying my heavy suitcase. Bread and meat cans rattling in it. Poppy staggering along.

When we got back up to the cemetery we had us another real surprise. Actually a couple surprises. One of the things was, there was a lot more people there on the gravestones than before. And they wasn't just sitting there looking at the ground, like before.

They was noisy and arguing. A few was tacking notes onto the trees, probably so relatives could maybe find them later. But mostly it was kids crying, mamas hollering. Men shouting and pushing each other. What was the reason for all this loud display, I wondered.

Then I saw the reason. Four huge big beer barrels set up for service on the gravestones. Bungs all started. People drinking beer out of pots and pans and cups and glasses. Fast as they could get it out of those barrels.

Then I saw Mama and the two little ones.

TERY: Had Grover disappeared by now? [I should not have interrupted, for Mr. Kuhl expresses a bit of irritation at my intrusion.]

MR. KUHL: Grover never disappeared. I just sort of forgot about mentioning him over and over. What was important was that Mama had found two iron pots. One was pretty huge and had handles and a lid. The other one was smaller and had a long handle on it, but still looked heavy. But a heavy pot didn't bother Mama at all. She was so strong. The family was all drinking beer, too, taking turns out of the heavy-looking pot with the long handle.

Mama's face was almost as red as Poppy's. Grover looked sleepy, as usual.

"Don't get me started, Julius," Mama said, burping some and wiping the foam off of her lip with her sleeve. "There's no water and we was all just thirsty and hungry unto death. And then those nice drunkards brought us those barrels and pickles and pretzels. It's food. It's not like we ourselfs are being drunkards here."

Mama looked peeved, and we all knew it was not a good idea to argue Mama when she had on her Peeved Look. Especially if she was full of beer and pickles. Which was a rare occurrence for her, you might say—the beer, not the Peeved Look. Then when Mama finally looked Poppy straight in the face, she screamed.

She screaming didn't cause anybody around to quit drinking beer. There already was a good lot of screaming going on. But at least, after her scream, she was finally giving Poppy her Concerned Look.

So Poppy had to break down and tell her all about our adventure down on Market Street. And I started to horn in and recite about the wad of cash in Poppy's pocket, but Poppy told me to hush up. So my mind turned to thoughts of beer, since I was pretty thirsty again. I started to move over towards the barrels. Poppy reached out and pulled me back, setting me down beside him on a gravestone.

"Open up your suitcase, Junior," he said. So I did, and Poppy pulled up his pants leg and got out his leg-knife. He sliced up a loaf right there on the stone. Cut a can of meat open. Sliced it up and stuck the meat onto the bread. Passed the sangwidges around to us. To this day, if I eat a cornbeef sangwidge, I think about that day and how Poppy shared it out to us. Grover and the little ones hogged down pickles and pretzels, too.

People stopped hollering and pickle-eating and beer-drinking and gathered close, looking at us lip-smacking sangwidge eaters.

So then Poppy pulled back what was left of his sleeves as if he would cut up the other loaf. Probably all ready to give it away to the onlookers. "Cast your bread upon the water...," said Poppy, giving a holy-type quote meaning that a feller who has something ought to be generous about them who don't. But Mama grabbed the loaf and threw it back in my suitcase.

Mama said, "No need to go overboard with a bunch of drunkards."

Meaning, no need to be too generous with our grave-yard neighbors, just because they was hungry.

So Poppy mentioned out loud about our famous U.S. Army giving bread and meat cans away down on Van Ness. A lot of our fellow beer-drinkers rushed off in that direction.

Then, to wash down our sangwidges, we all had a few sips of the beer left in Mama's pot. From the way men had always smacked their lips and burped and said *aaaah* after they drank beer, I always thought that beverage must be mighty tasty. Like rootbeer or lemonade. I could hardly wait to get me a nip, since I was twelve years old and never had been able to sneak me a drop yet.

But no, this was bitter and made you gag, at first. After the fifth or sixth swallow it went down easier, y'know. And it was wet, which is what was important. But to this very day, I don't much like the taste of it.

TERY: You mentioned the man in the green vest.

MR. KUHL: I did? Oh that man. I knew I had forgot something. There he was all of a sudden. That Green-Vest man upped and sat down on the gravestone right next to Poppy. Taking his hat off, brushing it with his sleeve like a dude and setting that hat next to him. Making hisself right to home.

"Nice knife," he said, and reached for it, where it was laying on the stone.

"Keenest blade I ever had," said Poppy, not stopping the sneaky-looking feller from picking up Poppy's leg-knife and holding it like a lifelong knife-fighter.

"Probably would cut this nice lady's throat quick as a whistle, wouldn't you say?"

This was a surprising remark coming from practically a guest on your gravestone.

"Might do," said Poppy, looking a bit worried.

"Of course, you got a wad there in your pocket that you could use to get this here knife back."

Mama horned in from where she was sitting close by. "What wad is this man talking about, Julius?" Mama had on her Concerned Look again.

"Well, Mayor Schmitz went and passed a box around, and folks pitched in and...."

"Yer man here's got a big wad of bills in his pocket, and he don't want to share with a needy feller human bean."

"This is a fact, Julius?"

"About the wad or the sharing?"

Mama got on her Peeved Look. "Is this here individual threatening me with your knife, Julius?"

Poppy didn't answer, but the Green-Vest man did. "I'm just telling yer man here some facts of life." The Green-Vest man sneered a snaggle-toothed smile. He moved Poppy's knife from one hand to the other, and back again, like he was playing with it.

Poppy told a lie: "I just gave it all away, so I don't got any left, friend."

"Well, I been watching you all this time, and you didn't give it away at all. So I'm thinking maybe this feller's got something more valuable that he'd maybe like to see get its throat cut some." Green-Vest looked serious.

Poppy looked more worried. "There's a lot of people around here who wouldn't let that happen."

"There's a lot of people around here who wouldn't care a fig, so give it up, pilgrim." He pointed the blade at Poppy's pocket.

Mama smiled with all her teeth, a rare occurrence and a fact which surprised anybody who was noticing. "Well," she said, "you're out of luck, mister, on account of the army has just arrived," and she raised her chin sort of in the direction behind the Green-Vest man.

Naturally, he turned to see and, at that, Mama picked up her iron beer pot by the handle and bashed him one on the side of the head. She gave him such a fine vigorous smash I was reminded of the vaunted feats of Buttons Williams of the Baltimore Orioles, celebrated in tales told at my firehouse.

"I don't see the army," went Poppy, pushing the Green-Vest man's body aside and looking all around.

"You'll want to hog-tie him, Julius," said Mama. "Take the man's clothes off first, so you can use his belt and braces. Tie the knots nice and tight. Drag him over there behind that big monument so he don't offend anybody else's eyes." She smiled her Satisfied Smile. "And throw his coat and pants and hat — and that green vest — out into the street for some unfortunate person to pick up. I'll just take those nice slim boots of his."

Poppy fumbled some at his own long-johns top. Probably figuring to tear off some more to wrap up the Green-Vest man's bleeding scalp with. After a bit of thought and with Mama starting to give him her Eagle-eye Look, Poppy gave up on that idea and did as he had been told. The ex-Green-Vest man hadn't quite bit the dust. But he had bit off more than he could chew. He sure had lost his shirt.

It seemed that nobody around us had paid any attention to our plight. Or to Mama's solution. Or to Poppy's disposal deed. Everybody seemed busy with their beer and the bread and meat they were bringing back from the army. In fact, there was even some singing going on, even while you could see the flatbed dead-wagons rolling by with more late residents on their way to the civic plaza morgue.

This is an amazing fact I have learnt over and over throughout my life: People will find ways to amuse theirselfs. Even when buildings are falling down around them. Even when fire is coming closer and closer. Which it was.

It was now after noon. The blue sky was puffy with clouds of black smoke and gray smoke and white smoke. You could hear boat whistles hooting in the bay and dynamite booms down below us. Bells still clanged and bonged, mostly fire bells. But since there was no water pressure and the cisterns was all empty, the only thing the woreout firemen and their poor dear horses could do was chop stuff down and help the army blow up buildings.

"I think we need to go south," said Mama, "and get out of this city, soon as we can." She sighed and looked down in the dumps again. Probably thinking about her dead babies.

"I'll try and find us a buckboard to rent. But where to find a mule, I don't know." Poppy wagged his head. Looked beat as well as burnt.

"Well, Julius, they're running loose all over the street. Alls you need do is catch one." A practical woman, Mama was right again, since lots of horses and mules were trotting by, snorting and scared-looking. And who knew where their owner was? "Find us a horse in harness. That'll save some time." Mama now had on her Business Look. And that's what started us on our way out of The City and, after a while, brought us over here to Balona.

I think I'll sort of rest now.

TERY: Have you found your father's good gold watch, the one with the green fob?

MR. KUHL: Green fob? Oh. Well. I looked and looked. Maybe it slipped under the mattress there. Speaking of which, I should check up on old Kon Chaud. I'll put off my rest for a while. If you'll help me get down the hall there and check up on old Kon.

TERY: Happy to help.

~

Mr. Junior Kuhl unfolds his metal walker, and I hold his door open while he scuttles out and down the hallway, leaning forward like a racer over handlebars in the Tour de France. He moves with a noisy scraping sound and remarkable speed, but I catch up with him.

"Is Mr. Kon Chaud another relative of yours?"

"No blood relation. He's Kenworth's father-in-law."

"Ah," and I point out, "that makes Mr. Chaud the grandfather of Richie Kuhl."

"I guess you mean the fat boy. I don't much like that fat boy any more, y'know." Mr. Kuhl shakes his head rapidly. "Don't have a good family feeling about that one."

Mr. Kon Chaud's room is nearby, and Mr. Junior Kuhl pushes his way through the door without knocking. "Kon? Kon? You up yet? Lunchtime's over. Too bad, you missed out on all that great food." Mr. Kuhl winks at me.

Mr. Kon Chaud looks up from his chair by his window, in the same place as Mr. Kuhl's chair by Mr. Kuhl's window. Mr. Chaud has the same kind of bush obscuring his view of Balona that has continued to bother Mr. Kuhl.

Mr. Kon Chaud presents another surprise. I had calculated that Mr. Chaud is at least ten or fifteen years younger than Mr. Junior Kuhl, but Mr. Chaud looks much older than Mr. Kuhl. Mr. Chaud's face is wrinkled like an old cotton shirt awaiting an iron. His red-rimmed eyes seem sunken, his complexion dead white, his hairless scalp a contour map of crevices, lumps, warts, and bumps. Mr. Kon Chaud stares and nods and smiles. I think that

168

perhaps he is blind, for he appears not to recognize Mr. Junior Kuhl, despite Mr. Kuhl's loud greeting.

"I like to argue old Kon here, since he never answers back." Mr. Kuhl chuckles and seats himself on Mr. Chaud's bed. "Drawr up a chair here and watch this."

I do as I am told and sit.

Mr. Kuhl shouts: "How's things, Kon?"

Mr. Chaud's toothless mouth curves upward. He nods, chuckles, drools, looks at me, reaches a finger out as if he would claw one of my red stockings.

He's not blind.

"Your grandson been visiting lately? That fat boy?"

Mr. Chaud looks around the room, coughs, sniffs.

"He's my own great-grandson, y'know, that fat boy is."

Mr. Chaud, still smiling, hiccups.

"You got your jewelry and cash hid, Kon?"

No response.

"Can I check under your mattress?" Mr. Junior Kuhl moves as if to raise part of Mr. Chaud's mattress.

Mr. Chaud squeals. Loudly. And he squeals again and his smile disappears. He looks pained.

Mr. Kuhl says, "See, he's not totally gone yet. Just about, though." Mr. Kuhl shakes his head and indicates Mr. Chaud with his thumb. "I don't want to go like this. I want to go in a blaze of glory." He snakes his hand toward Mr. Chaud's mattress once again. Mr. Chaud squeals, this time much more loudly.

Kevin peers into the room. "Okay in here?"

Mr. Junior Kuhl ignores the question.

"Well, as usual," observes Kevin.

"See, girl," says Mr. Kuhl, "old Kon here's got his own opera-soprano burglar alarm system. Only problem is, I keep hearing it in the middle of the night.

"Maybe he's got wraiths, too. Think about that, will you."

I follow Mr. Kuhl back to his room. He travels much more slowly this time. Still in his robe, he climbs into his bed, pulls the sheet up to his chin as if he is experiencing a chill. "So, now you got some more idears." Mr. Kuhl closes his eyes.

He opens one eye. "We just about finished, are we? You got my brain all squoze out? Well, come back again, and let's finish up. I'm about wore to a frazzle." He closes the eye and begins snoring at once.

I leave wondering if we have a can of corned beef at home. I would make Mr. Junior Kuhl a nice, reminiscence-type sandwich for his after-supper snack—lots of mayonnaise.

16

Editor insists on greater effort by reporter

At home, after finding a can of corned beef in a cupboard, and getting Penny's approval to donate it to Mr. Junior Kuhl's welfare, I sit in the kitchen and watch Penny start supper. My mother was a good cook, but Penny uses herbs and spices that I doubt Mommy ever used. Penny's food tastes different. Not better or worse, just different.

Of course, I was five years old the last time I tasted Mommy's cooking, so I am only estimating here. I have to admit that Penny is a pretty good cook. I notice that Daddy likes her cooking and compliments her about it often, obviously respects her cooking ability. Hugs her a lot, too.

Although I intend to be a scholar-adventurer-journalist with sailboating and horseback-riding as hobbies, and perhaps an airplane-piloting forensic psychiatrist with martial arts as a continuing interest, I have been thinking that maybe I should ask Penny to teach me some recipes. I have seen that many big-time TV chefs are male. Davy

Narsood, for example. But effective modern women need to know how to prepare food that tastes good. We cannot leave important achievement to men only.

I might eventually be able to produce something as tasty as Penny does. Daddy would compliment me and respect me, maybe give me a hug once in a while. I'll have to plan how to ask.

I am thinking such thoughts as I respond to our doorbell. Framed in the screendoor with the afternoon sun behind it, the silhouette is obviously Sheba's. Before letting her in, I close the big wooden sliding doors leading to the dining room, so that Penny won't be bothered.

Sheba speaks, "I just thought long as I was like in the neighborhood, I should ought to drop by and check up on your progress, since you didn't show up for a pep-talk this afternoon."

I ask Sheba in, and we seat ourselves on one of the new couches Penny bought to please Daddy. Sheba usually wears a lot of bright lipstick. Her lipstick is green today, and smeared off to one side of her mouth. Her arm is held across her chest in a sling fashioned from what looks like a flowered apron.

"I could've like used my new cellphone and called you up first, but I decided I should drop in and check up on your progress. See here?" Sheba holds up her free arm and displays a small instrument strapped to her wrist. "It's a wrist phone but it takes pictures and records messages. My cellphone does. If you don't mind me saying so, you ought to have one. All my reporters ought to get one. This one was gave to me by my step-dad. I mean, you don't need that old notebook once you got one of these."

Sheba holds up the phone arm again and waves it about, allowing us to view the instrument from various angles.

The couch cushions squeak and groan as she repositions her body several times.

"Big couch," she observes. "Probably costed a mint. But then you guys are filthy rich, so who cares. You like didn't ask me about my arm."

"You hurt your arm."

"I wasn't the one did it. I shouldn't tell anybody, but I'll tell you, since you're now my subordinate on my staff. Richie's the one did it. Right next door there on your corner." Sheba gestures with her thumb. "Not like *on* the corner. In his house, actually, after the sheriffs left." Sheba leans toward me to explain. "I'm an investigative reporter, y'know, not just an editor. So I was watching from a distance and saw Richie and Pee take off. And like Richie saw me. And as soon as the sheriffs left we both like went back to his house. Richie told my brother to get lost."

"So Richie is home now?"

Sheba's eyes narrow. "I don't know where he is now."

"Do you hurt?"

"I been hurting all my life, child. A little arm-twist isn't gonna ruin my life. My boyfriend in tragedy is the problem. He needs me to support him, not pick on him, like he said a couple times this afternoon. He goes like, 'How come you're over here?' and I, like, 'I'm here to support you,' but he didn't like my answer.

"'You're gonna betray me to the pigs,' he goes. He calls the cops pigs, like on the TV. 'No,' I go. I like, 'I could've called 'em on my new cellphone here.' I held my arm up so he could see. I like, 'I could've told 'em where you are. But I didn't.' Then Richie tries to grab my cellphone ."

"I guess he didn't get it," I say.

"Well, like you can see here, the thing's strapped on good and tight. You can take pictures with it, y'know. You get a special thing to stick into it and you can send a fax and get on the stock market. I had to go over to Runcible's in the Mall and learn how to use it, y'know?" Sheba lowers her voice. "Saleslady told me confidentally I could get all the porn I want, just by pushing buttons on here. Showed me how. Wears out the battery fast but. You can't do that with Richie's phone." Sheba sniffs.

"Richie did that to your arm?"

"He tried to grab my cellphone off of my wrist. Actually, you don't need to know this part. This is a need-to-know thing, like they say on the TV. Need-to-know. But if you don't mind me saying so, you're a junior member of my own staff, so I guess it's okay if you know. I got to thinking, probably me and Richie could like get on TV and tell our tragic story, make some fame and cash that way?"

"Probably Buddy Swainhammer would put you on his radio show and you could tell everybody in Chaud County."

"I didn't think about that one. You couldn't see us live and in color that way, but radio would work, second-best." Sheba contemplates, possibly figuring audience responses. "Yeah, Richie did it again, twisted my arm. Better than hitting, y'know. I felt his wrath. He's so strong."

Sheba's green lips move from side to side. "But not strong enough to get my new phone away from me." Sheba chortles at that, providing a passable rendition of The Wicked Witch of the West. The green lipstick perhaps helps with the impression.

I should bite my tongue.

"You can tell where you are, too," she adds, "only I haven't figured out how to do that." She thinks briefly. "Maybe I could ask Richie. And you can multiply and subtract if you can figure out what buttons to push."

"You said you dropped in to check on my progress."

Sheba frowns. "You're not interested in my tragedy?"

"I believe you're competent to take care of it yourself. You're not likely to ask the assistance of a younger, less experienced person, a subordinate. I doubt I could be of much help in a love tragedy, and you already know that."

I smirk internally.

Sheba looks relieved. "Yeah. If you don't mind me saying so, you're like too young to understand these sex-related things that got me and Richie all upset." She holds her phone up to her eyes, appears to thumb in some code, unstraps the instrument, and hands it to me.

"You can take my picture in my painful situation. Get some of this couch in the picture, too, so I can show my ma where I actually was. Maybe I'll put it in the *Korndogger*, to show how us editors strive for our readers."

After she shows me which button to push, Sheba poses and I snap two shots. The little phone has its own built-in flash unit. Then Sheba does something with the phone and we are more-or-less able to see the photos that appear on the tiny screen. She seems delighted. "It's digital, see, where little pixies like make up the picture. Look at that. I look like a soldier there, don't I."

She pulls the sling up over her head, folds it, and stuffs it into her backpack. "I thought I might have like a cracked bone, here, or a sprain, but it's already fine now." Buckling the phone back on her wrist, Sheba finally asks, "So, how's your crappy old-guy story coming? Still no good?"

She sniffs.

Sniffs yet again.

I answer, "It's about ready to wrap up. In his tale, Mr. Junior Kuhl has just about survived the earthquake and fire and soon will be on his way to Balona. That is, I believe that is what's likely to happen. He lives here now, and it appears obvious that the family must have escaped San Francisco."

"Well, the old guy had a little tragedy, all right, maybe. I only hope that you can like write it up so that kids won't fall asleep reading about it." Sheba wags her head. "I actually doubt you can like do anything with old guy material."

I shrug. "Do my best," I say.

"I don't wanna have to spike it. But I will if I have to. If it's not good enough." Sheba sniffs one more time, perhaps for emphasis.

I hold the door open for Sheba and follow her onto the porch. As she trudges down the steps, walking toward First Avenue and disappearing around the corner, she keeps her head turned toward the Kuhl house. Probably Richie is still at home.

But I decide to let things happen naturally. The law will get Richie sooner or later.

Everybody says so.

17

Refugees invent unique way to honor president

Mr. Junior Kuhl's first word as he unwraps my offering is, "Yum." He then demonstrates his enthusiasm for my corned beef sandwich creation by cramming the sections into his mouth, not quite all of them at once. I am at first concerned that he might strangle, but with both cheeks bulging and eyes sparkling and head nodding in time to his mastications and swallowings, he appears happier than I have ever seen him.

He manages to croak, "This sangwidge hits the spot."

"I mixed the corned beef with plenty of mayonnaise, as you said you like it that way. It's supposed to be better with chopped-up onions, but I guessed those would be harder to chew."

Mr. Kuhl continues to nod and smile, settles back in his chair, sighs. "I wisht I had that sangwidge every day."

He closes his eyes, appears about to take a nap, but then jerks awake. "I forgot to mention the horse."

"Ah, your favorite firehorse."

MR. JUNIOR KUHL: No, no. It was the horse that Poppy went out into the street and stopped. A fine roan gelding with a white blaze and white socks, like long-johns peeping out there. You know what a gelding is?

TERY: I think so.

MR. KUHL: Well, then, I won't go into that, since you're a lady and all. Anyways, this beautiful big horse was a carriage horse. You could see how it was a regular carriage horse. Since it was carrying a whole lot of harness. And dragging nice traces. Looked like it had ran off from its carriage-house.

Scared, maybe. You'd maybe be scared, too, if a building was collapsing on you and a huge big fire was whomping itself up at you.

TERY: [I agree with a nod.]

MR. KUHL: "So," said Poppy, "we got us a volunteer horse." He stroked the horse on its blaze. And the horse looked at Poppy. Stood there stamping its feet a little, whinnied some, snorted. Going nowhere, like it was grateful to be in a nice cool graveyard with no fire around or falling bricks.

First the horse nuzzled Poppy a little. Like it was telling Poppy it was a horse sure to be friendly to humans—or else that it was hungry. Then the horse started nibbling on grave grass. One thing about a horse. Even if it's got a bit in its mouth, it'll nibble on stuff to eat. I guess it's kind of like being able to chew DubbleBubble and eat a korndog at the same time. Balona kids still learn how to do that, right?

TERY: Sounds authentic.

MR. KUHL: Mama right away said that Poppy needed to find us a buckboard. You know what a buckboard is?

TERY: [I spread my hands, as if puzzled.]

MR. KUHL: A buckboard is a four-wheel wagon pulled by a horse or a mule. No top over it. But you hope it's got springs. If you're lucky, it's got a box around the bed with sides maybe a foot high. So your goods or kids don't slide off. And you can maybe sleep in it at night. It's got maybe a nice bench seat up front. Where you can sit all grand. Tell your horse where to go.

It looked like the ferryboat was a bad bet for us. Everybody around us was saying that the railroad tracks was all bent out of shape for miles. Except we found out later that wasn't totally true. So a buckboard is what we needed, all right. Mama had figured that out quick as a wink. But, far as you could see through the smoke and flames, there was bricks and trash and people and animals scurrying in the road. But no abandoned buckboard in sight.

Poppy said to Mama, "You can ride up on this here horse with the little ones for a while, and me and the boys'll walk aside you, and we'll all keep our eyes peeled for a spare buckboard nobody's using."

Poppy was the most honest man I ever knew. Except that right then he sounded a lot like he was telling us to look out for somebody else's buckboard that we could take for our own.

Poppy thought for a while, looking at me and Grover. "Of course," he said, patting at his derringer coat pocket, "now we got us a few dollars ahead, maybe I could buy us a buckboard. Off of somebody who didn't need his."

"You got to find one first." That was Mama reminding us to do something important. She always did that.

So, what would you do when you got a family with a hungry and thirsty wife and kids. And you could see all those people running by, scared and hungry and thirsty. And their houses burnt or collapsed-down. And not enough clothes on. Some even barefoot. And no money to spend. And nowhere to go. And fires like tigers, burning bright. And probably more earthquake to come. But then you finally find you a nice, big horse with harness attached to it. And you got some bread and cans of meat. In a suitcase your fine son is still carrying. What to do?

TERY: Check on the ferry boat again.

MR. KUHL: No, I already said about that. What you do is you look for that buckboard. Grover was whining. So Mama right away said, "Grover's got a sore foot. He needs to ride up on the horse there with me.

So Poppy went and hiked Mama and Grover and the little ones up on the horse. Naturally, there was no saddle. But that fine horse had a broad back. Comfortable, too, it looked like. Poppy folded up the harness. Wrapped the reins so they wouldn't hang down and trip the horse. He said that Grover was now in charge of the harness and not to drop any piece of it. Grover whined some more. Complained about his foot. But then he more or less did what Poppy said. Poppy looked at me and my suitcase and said I should hand it up to Grover.

"How come?" I said. "I'm the one found it. It's not Grover's suitcase. It's mine." I was probably sounding like Grover, whining.

"Well, then," said Poppy, "you want to carry it, go ahead and carry it."

"And here," said Mama, "Junior can carry this, too. It'll come in handy down the road." She hung onto the water pot with beer in it, but she handed Poppy her huge big heavy iron pot with the long handle. The one she bashed Green-Vest with. Poppy made me open up my suitcase. I had to stuff that pot in. Empty, but talk about heavy.

This was a lesson for me that I never forgot. Since that suitcase got heavier. And heavier as we walked out of the graveyard and down past a lot of fires and wild sights and towards the south of the city. From that one lesson I learned to listen to Poppy more. Not be so ready to contradict him right away. Which is what many offsprings will do to their fine elders.

My own boys used to contradict me all the time. And they wasn't even carrying suitcases. I hope you don't contradict your elders.

TERY: I try never to contradict my elders.

MR. KUHL: You do make a good sangwidge, too. You'll be a fine catch for some deserving feller some day. Although maybe you answer back too quick.

TERY: I'll try to do better.

MR. KUHL: See what I mean? Well, anyways, there we was. A little family, Grover whining. Mama commenting about Poppy's rosy complexion. The little ones sniveling.

Little ones will snivel, y'know, no matter what. Unless you amuse them all the time. Nowadays you got the TV to park them in front of. Let them learn everything they need to know about life from. But in the old days there wasn't no such blessed TV. You just had to bear up under all that sniveling. And teach the kiddies about life all by yourself. Soon turned Poppy's hair snow white. As you can see, I inherited Poppy's hair color.

But there is some advantage to having kids. Which I figured out some later: When you have kids, you live forever. Anyways, everybody watched us as we took off out of the graveyard. Some commenting on how they wisht they had a horse. We all looked straight ahead. And for a while I carried my suitcase on my head like an African native carries pots. Until that suitcase got to rubbing all the hair off of my scalp. I practically got bald-headed.

Then I tried carrying it over my shoulder until my arm near fell off. I had found a nice belt in the street, so I took that belt and rigged a sling. That worked for a while. But since we walked a long, long way, my suitcase got heavier and heavier. Every once and a while I would look back.

The farther away we got away from the city, the more our beautiful San Francisco looked like a big flaming, smoking trash pile.

Pretty soon we came acrost another group of people where the fires hadn't got to, and maybe would skip. This time the group was mostly ladies with aprons. "We come from over west on the coast," said a short fat lady in boots. She wore her apron on top of bib overalls like my overalls, only a whole lot bigger. Waving her hand towards the ocean side of the city, she told us, "Our houses didn't all fall down. Some did, but we got only a couple little fires over there, so Rachel here and Margaret said we should ought to do some Christian work. Except Rachel is a Jewish lady and didn't exactly mention about Christian work. Anyways, we quick collected all these nice clothes and things from our neighbors and brought them over."

And there beside the road these ladies had a team of horses. And a huge big wagon full of clothes and things. I wouldn't say they was exactly *nice* clothes and things. But if you wore one, you wouldn't freeze or cause a caution. We didn't need any clothes. But Grover whined that his foot hurt. And the nice Jewish lady went "Awww, you sweet boy," which is what ladies always did say to Grover. She handed him up a pair of heavy socks. Too big, but a nice thought. Grover didn't say thanks. Just grabbed that kind offering.

Grover was always like that. But people seemed to like him. Maybe they confused him with me, since we looked the same. Daisy liked him. A whole lot.

TERY: Sorry to interrupt, but you said you and Grover *looked* the same?

MR. KUHL: Like I said before, we was twins. Identical. Only we wore different clothes. Saw the whole world different. I was a leader and he wasn't. Wasn't much of a follower, either. Let's forget Grover and get back to important things. I mentioned the nice fat lady?

Well, the nice fat lady gazed worried at Poppy. "You look like you might be coming down with the measles," she said. She sneaked a quick peek at Poppy's exposed belly. She handed him a wrinkled white shirt without the collar, normal shirt style in those days. "You could slip it on later, when there's no ladies around," she said. Poppy tipped what was left of his hat, looked pleased.

Nobody gave me a thing. But then I didn't whine.

"Could you maybe use a hat?" went the fat lady, still looking at Poppy. Like everybody else, she had probably noticed the miserable sight that was left sitting on top of Poppy's head.

"Well, ma'am, I guess I could," went Poppy, all polite.

It turned out there was no hat that Poppy would choose for hisself, but a man had to have a hat in those day. If a man didn't wear a hat, people would be shocked, since the hatless feller looked right naked. So, when the lady handed him a huge big Mexican sombrero, Poppy went and took it, with thanks.

We all chuckled a lot. The hat wasn't real clean. It had dingles hanging all around the brim, like little gold balls.

But Poppy wore that hat till he d-i-d-e. Everybody in Balona called him "Saneyor Kuhl." Nowadays, he would have to carry a guitar with him. Play at weddings.

TERY: [I think Mr. Kuhl was making a joke, of sorts.]

MR. KUHL: Then I noticed Poppy looking hard at the wagon holding the clothes.

But it was Mama, thinking ahead again who said, "You by any chance got some blankets?"

"Why sure," said the Christian lady, and handed up Mama a thin blanket for each of us. And sort of a nice quilt, to boot. Mama rolled those blankets up around each little kid and herself and Grover.

Lucky we had a big horse.

"Bless your hearts," said Poppy to all the nice ladies.

"Tell your personal servant he can stuff this here blanket into the suitcase there," said Mama to Poppy, passing the thing to him, who passed it to me. When she said *personal servant*, she meant me, of course. I don't know why.

Which I went and did. And which made my suitcase even heavier. But which kept Mama's pot from bonking on the cans inside. By that time, I was hoping we'd find a buckboard real soon.

"Could there be a food wagon about, too?" said Poppy, probably having gave up on noticing the clothes wagon. Which he surely had been thinking about buying with his hero reward money.

"Yes, indeedy, right down the road there, if it isn't et up already. Grocers donerated food stuff and been giving it away off of their auto truck like it was going out of style."

Can you see that it wasn't everybody who was out for hisself or looting or cutting off fingers? Yes, there was mostly a lot of good people. Helping each other. San Francisco always been proud of their kind people.

184

Poppy said, "Could there be a buckboard about, too? One nobody seems to want? Sort of a spare buckboard left to the elements?" Poppy was pushing kind of hard, but the ladies all was shaking their heads no. No spare buckboard around.

Well, then, we proceeded along. Having the fine tail and broad rump of this horse in my direct view, it occurred to me that we didn't know its name.

I hollered at Poppy. "This here horse probably has got a name," I said.

Poppy stopped and swayed like he'd been struck by lightning. The horse stopped, too, of course. Everybody looked surprised that we had a horse we didn't know the name of. "Yes," said Poppy, "this horse has got to have a name." He looked at the horse. Then looked at each of us. "What name do you think would be a nice name for this excellent beast?"

We all thought a while.

Mama was still looking glum and said it didn't make any difference to her, but we ought to get going so we could find shelter before the sun went down. Grover didn't even think about it, since he was still busy trying to pull on his new socks without falling off of the horse. The little ones didn't know what we were talking about. So it was up to me and Poppy to name the horse.

I said, "How's about we name this horse after our famous president?"

Poppy snapped his fingers. Said that was the best idear he'd ever heard and, "We'll call him Theodore."

"But everybody calls our president Teddy," I said. And Poppy right away agreed that we should call our fine beast Teddy. And so Teddy it was. As I recall, Teddy agreed by making a horse noise that most of us laughed about. But naming Teddy made us think like we had done an actual accomplishment. And we all felt better, me especially, since it was my idear in the first place.

Good idear?

TERY: [I nod agreement, vigorously.]

MR. KUHL: Well, then, soon we came acrost another wagon. This one not a horse wagon, but a new flat-bed auto truck painted a bright, shiny black, but with muddy wheels. The kind of truck that ran on gasoline and made a lot of noise and an awful smell. Probably a rich farmer owns it, we thought.

The auto truck was loaded with crates that probably used to hold carrots and onions and radishes. There was only a few of those vegetables showing. And a crowd of people was waiting for the leftovers.

So we watched for a while, but didn't get much closer to the tasty stuff that was making my stomach rumble.

I'd have preferred cans of meat, but the thought of biting into a nice fat onion was uncorking a geyser in my mouth.

"Let's get a move on, Julius," said Mama, so Poppy did as he was told, leading Teddy. Me tottering along behind, under the awful weight of my suitcase.

"You poor struggling lad," said a roly-poly man sitting in a chair at the side of the road. He was doing nothing labor-like. But he was sweating and kept wiping his forehead with what used to be a red bandana. "If you want, you could use this here barrow that somebody has abandoned."

And sure enough, people did leave things to the elements. For right there was an old wheelbarrow. Dirt spilled out of it, turned over at the roadside. Just waiting for somebody to claim it and call it his own.

186

Nowadays, wheelbarrows got balloon tires that you could rush nitroglycerine around in. They're so gentle on the road. This old barrow had a bare iron wheel that vibrated so my teeth jounced together over every pebble. Caused my teeth to fall out early. I'll show you. See here? But the barrow was mine.

Poppy nodded his head and thanked the man. I remembered to thank the man, too. So I righted my barrow, heaved my suitcase into it. And off we went, Poppy walking and holding onto the bridle, Teddy keeping the family atop, and me commanding my clanking vehicle, guarding the rear against unpleasant surprises.

18

Balona pioneer's narration holds reporter enthralled

"It's deadline, so where's your story?" Sheba seems to be imposing an arbitrary conclusion to my assignment.

I feel like coughing, my toe like tapping. "Well, I can have it for you tomorrow or the next day."

"No. Too late." Sheba sniffs. "I got to have it now. Right this minute, actually."

I do cough and my foot taps spontaneously, not all that discreetly. She peers into my face, checks out my toes, and performs her one-sided smirk. "Well, I could still accept it tomorrow. But I got to have plenty of time to work it over, change it where it needs."

Mr. Peralta looks up from his papers. "I'm interested, too, Tery. Tomorrow will be fine. If you're ready."

"I already told the kid."

"Yes, I heard, Sheba. Tomorrow will be fine."

I cannot help sighing. "I'd like to put some finishing touches on it, but tomorrow's fine with me, too." I gather my notes, smile to myself, for I am indeed pretty much finished. All I need is a sort of conclusion. I'll try to get Mr. Kuhl to describe quickly the family's escape from San Francisco and their journey to Balona. The major part of his story is the earthquake and fire, and those adventures are all ready to go.

~

I get to Mr. Junior Kuhl's room right after the Jolly Times lunch hour. He attends to my offering at once.

"Young woman, did I ever tell you that you make a fine, tasty sangwidge?"

Although I appreciate a compliment as much as anyone, I want to move the interview along and meet Sheba's deadline. "I'm impressed with how you have described your fine horse, Mr. Kuhl. But by now, Teddy must have a grave somewhere around Balona."

MR. KUHL: Well now, everybody liked Teddy. He passed over when he was maybe twenty-five. A good long life for a horse. Just didn't get up onto his feet one morning. The way I feel most mornings lately. But if you got any business sense at all, you never bury a horse. Oh, rich folks might do that with a famous thoroughbred that got his picture in the paper. Put a cross up over his grave. Bring flowers, say a prayer, that sort of thing.

[Mr. Kuhl looks at the ceiling.] What was I saying?

TERY: Burying a horse?

MR. KUHL: No, no. You don't bury a horse. Somebody with any business sense at all calls up the rendering plant over at Fruitstand. They come with their huge big smelly truck. Haul his dead body off.

TERY: Rendering.

MR. KUHL: Make him into horsehide. For shoes and jackets and furniture. And dogfood. And glue. Of course, you could also call up a slaughterhouse for him. They'd like him.

TERY: [Mr. Kuhl looks at me as if I might not believe him.]

MR. KUHL: Oh, yes. There's lots of people around, here and in foreign lands, crave nice red rare horseflesh on their plate.

TERY: [I swallow hard.] A sad end for a loyal friend.

MR. KUHL: Maybe sad, but natural. Maybe useful. Good to be useful. Everything's got a beginning. And a middle and an end. Including friends. Including parents and brothers and sisters. Just you think about San Francisco. All those buildings fell down and burnt up. All those people there surprised as all get-out to go w-e-s-t.

Horses and dogs and cats and rats burnt up, too. Not to speak of my tiny baby sister and brother. That was all a big waste. But it was a natural end. Not useful, probably, but natural.

TERY: But when Teddy died I suppose your Poppy was sad about losing a friend.

MR. KUHL: Poppy would've went and dug a huge big hole in the backyard. Put up a cross. Brought flowers. But it wasn't Poppy called up the rendering. It was Mama. Mama always did the stuff Poppy didn't have a mind to do."

TERY: I suppose women are stronger.

MR. KUHL: Not stronger, girl. Meaner.

TERY: Oh. [I don't know how to respond to that. It is a question I have pondered before. Are women stronger in times of crisis, or are they only more "practical"? About the subject Mr. Kuhl seems to have an attitude.]

MR. KUHL: Anyways, we all did cry, Poppy especially. Even Mama had on her Concerned Look. But Teddy wasn't wasted. Besides, Teddy didn't know one way or the other. He was useful all his life. Then one day when he was real old, he just up and d-i-d-e. Didn't I already say? Surprised us all, but he was still useful after he went west. Mama got a nice pocketful of change out of it.

TERY: It's still sad, unless perhaps you have religion and believe you'll meet someday in Heaven.

MR. KUHL: Religion is bushwa.

TERY: Bush...what?

MR. KUHL: ...wa. Bushwa. Hogwash would be a nice way to put it.

TERY: Well, Mr. Kuhl, a good many people would disagree.

MR. KUHL: A good many people will disagree about everything. Still don't make 'em right. But just because you don't get down on your knees every night don't mean you won't meet again. I could tell you something about that. I could tell you about me and somebody already gone w-e-s-t having regular meetings.

Only you wouldn't believe me. [Mr. Kuhl smiles.]

Say, I haven't had a decent argument like this in years. Too bad it's so late.

TERY: It's only two.

MR. KUHL: I mean late for me, since I'm ending. Yep, I feel it coming on. Oh, don't look like that. Fare-thee-wells are sad only if you think they're going to be sad. If I was sick and painful. Or out of it like old Kon Chaud down the hall. Then I'd be happy for it. Actually, I do kind of look forward to meeting old Lucifer. Finally get warm. Get it over with, y'know, and make room for another genera-tion. [Mr. Kuhl raises his eyebrows at me.] That's the way it has to be, or there'll be too many people. But pity I'll never be useful. The way old Teddy was.

Mr. Kuhl freezes, slaps his knee, chuckles, looks up at me out of the corner of his eye. From his expression, I am absolutely sure that he is thinking about changing his will so that he himself can be sent over to Fruitstand to be rendered. His chest jumps as he laughs silently, bobbles his head, probably considering exactly that scenario.

In the few seconds that Mr. Kuhl chuckles, I think about Mommy and how she lay in pain for such a long time, trapped in that snake's nest of plastic tubes. I have always wondered if she welcomed her ending. She remained silent recently when I asked her about that, but I remember her moaning repeatedly back then, "Let me go." Then she was gone. Jack keeps saying the same thing to me about lettng Mommy go. But I've been seeing how joyful Mr. Kuhl is at a hundred-five, happy to still be in touch with his Poppy.

Needing to change the subject from rendering, I take a breath and interrupt with a stupid but journalistically necessary question: "Mr. Kuhl, I'm supposing that you finally did come across a buckboard?"

MR. KUHL: What about crossing a blackboard?

TERY: Buckboard.

MR. KUHL: Oh, that. A few miles down the peninsula, there it was. My suitcase was a huge big chore to bus by this time, even in my wheelbarrow. Then we saw it. This nice old splintery buckboard with a crooked wheel. Sitting there abandoned. Sort of.

TERY: Sort of abandoned?

MR. KUHL: Well, there wasn't nobody minding it. And the house next to it looked abandoned, too, when Poppy hollered at it.

TERY: So you took it then and there?

MR. KUHL: Feller came out of the house scratching hisself whilst Poppy was giving that buckboard a real close look. So Poppy made him an offer. Then Mama gave a big loud sigh. Made the feller her own offer. Whilst Poppy counted out the cash, the owner looked like he wisht he'd held out for more.

Teddy backed into the shafts and got hooked up like he was borned to it. Which he was, of course.

TERY: So you finally had transportation for the entire family.

MR. KUHL: Almost the entire family. For them as was left anyways.

TERY: Mr. Kuhl, do you wish you'd done anything in your life differently?

MR. KUHL: [He looks at the ceiling, then at the wall, then at me.] Now that you mention it, I do wisht I had done a few things different.

I wisht I'd been a hero once and a while. Instead of always considering the odds. I was a businessman, y'know. [Mr. Kuhl sighs.] I wisht my mama loved me. Like she always loved Grover. I wisht Daisy loved me instead of my money.

[Mr. Kuhl searches under his robe, probably for the missing locket. He lifts his chin and inhales loudly.] I wisht I could run faster than Grover. Grover complained every day of his life about his athlete's foot problem, but he always beat me at running.

I wisht I'd had a dog. I never had a dog. Mama always said dogs was dirty and smelled bad. So I never got one. Then Daisy had a cat. Brought it with her to the marriage bed. Said she didn't want to disturb her cat's personality. Cat used to bite me every chance it got. When the Grim Reaper finally come calling for that cat—seemed like it lived a hundred years — I thought a lot about shipping it off to Fruitstand where I might get Daisy a nice furpiece out of the deal. And they could extract catgut, eksedra, make musicians happy. But Daisy went and dug the hole in the backyard herself. Banged together a wood cross over it. Flowers on it. Went out there and talked to it every night.

That part I can understand.

TERY: [My pulse and respiration are increasing, for I don't want to hear any more of Mr. Kuhl's observations about rendering.]

MR. KUHL: [He suddenly turns to face me. He shakes his head.] I got no business talking stuff like that to a young thing just starting out in life.

TERY: Well, it is interesting.

[Another matter could prove interesting, but I decide not to share with Mr. Kuhl my own ability to converse across dimensions. Readers of the *Korndogger* would find the subject to be pure fantasy.]

MR. KUHL: Girl, you just got to remember that death is a natural thing. We go about our business fat and happy. But old Death is always with us tapping his foot. Just the way you tap your foot there once and a while. He's looking at the fine gold watch he stole from me, the one with the green fob.

[Mr. Kuhl points at shards of wallpaper.] See? He's right there waiting for us. Smiling. So I say don't worry about it, but you better try to live a good life where you treat people nice. And always have your emergency bag filled up. And don't forget the water bottle. What was I saying?

TERY: Water?

MR. KUHL: Ah. Besides the crooked wheel, that's what gave us the most trouble on the big trip. We had to go all the way around the bay. A long trip, and bay water is salt water. Can't drink it. Had to keep our eyes peeled for any good water. We went down the peninsula and acrost and then up over the hills. And down into the big valley. We had picked up vegetables and more bread from farms along the way. Even a cake. Stale, but tasty. Grover kept snacking on it, Mama not saying a word about snacking.

And Poppy got to milk a lost cow. Impressive when you didn't know Poppy had such talent. "Same technique as with a goat," went Poppy. who when a boy tended goats. Squirted quite a few swallows right into Mama's pot, before the cow kicked Poppy's knee and ran away. But that didn't last long. Grover slurped up most of that fine fresh drink. We had went through Mama's beer pot pretty quick, so it was the thirst that kept getting to us.

Took us eight days to get to Balona. Lucky we had old Teddy. Lucky we got that buckboard, crooked wheel and all. Lucky it was springtime and rained some or we might've been mummies out there in the weeds. Lucky Poppy was finally lucky.

TERY: You were all by yourselves on the road?

MR. KUHL: Lordy, no. Lots of traffic, like today. Terrible road, not like the fine freeways now. Mostly dirt and gravel then, and rocks and mud. But lots of traffic. Big ruts in the road. Loud autocars blasting through once and a while, klaxons scaring the horses. Hogging the roadway. Or else broke down and the drivers whining for help. Not so stuck-up then. Hungry-thirsty travelers all. Mostly people escaping from the quake and fire.

Always people at the side of the road selling something. Trying to take advantage. Lucky Poppy still had some cash and bought us an old shovel so we could dig little holes and cover up our people-pucky, since we had to do it wherever we could. You didn't have your service station on the side of the road back then.

TERY: You pushed your wheelbarrow all the way to Balona?

MR. KUHL: I don't wish! Poppy wanted to leave it at the side of the road somewheres so I could ride. Mama said to bring it up onto the buckboard. "We can trade something for it," Mama said. "Junior can walk," she said. But I opened up the tailgate. Heaved the barrow up and squeezed my way onto the back of the rig. Mama gave me her Eagle Look, but I jounced there for most of the trip. At night, I clonked my barrow off onto the ground. It was my private bunkbed. With my quilt over me I was snug as a bug in a rug. Grover was blue jealous.

TERY: I guess you got to Balona without too much trouble.

MR. KUHL: Oh, we had trouble, all right. But one of our family members pretty much got us out of it. [Mr. Kuhl is wearing a sly look now. A secret up his sleeve perhaps.]

TERY: Your mother solved another problem, I bet.

MR. KUHL: You maybe remember the Green-Vest Man. [Mr. Kuhl opens his robe and points his thumb at the place where one wears a vest.]

TERY: Your mama bashed him with the beer pot, and you left him in the cemetery.

MR. KUHL: There we was, Poppy and Teddy walking at a nice clip, the rest of us crowded on the buckboard. We was starting up the steep hill towards where the famous bandido Joaquin Murieta and his gang was supposed to hang out in old times. [Mr. Kuhl closes his robe and pulls it about himself more tightly.] I was kind of hoping we'd meet us some road agents, since every kid learned to read so he could handle penny dreadfuls and find out about road agents who would rob travelers and leave 'em in the lurch.

TERY: I guess those days weren't all that different from today, when we have carjackers in Delta City.

MR. KUHL [ignoring my contribution]: Road agents sometimes went in a group riding together. Four or five on horseback. They would rob travelers and then split up and go their separate ways. Then you'd have to get a posse together and go after those desperados.

TERY: Did you ever have to do that, Mr. Kuhl?

MR. KUHL: So there we was, innocent lambs. [He peers at me.] You following this, are you?

TERY: [I nod.]

MR. KUHL: There was this clump of oaks at the side of the road a few yards in front of us. There wasn't nobody before or behind us. And no birds sang. A dark cloud right overhead. Very strange. Usually there was birds everywhere and lots of traffic on the road, like I mentioned. Didn't I mention that?

TERY: [I nod again, noticing a definite change in Mr. Kuhl's delivery. He is almost singing his words, sermon-like.]

MR. KUHL: Suddenly, [he jumps in his chair, startling me] out from behind the trees there appears in front of us this figure on horseback. Appears like a wraith. Sort of fog surrounding him. Holding a horse pistol, which is a huge big sidearm carried by cal'vrymen. He is pointing this horse pistol straight at me. [Mr. Kuhl sits up straight, shouts now.] The feller hollers, "Stand and deliver. Gim'me that hero cash." We was thunderstruck, since it was the Green-Vest Man, now returned from the cemetery, come back for revenge, and threatening us, life and limb. [Mr.

Kuhl wags his head sadly.] And Mama's beerpot there in my suitcase

TERY: So you were robbed on your way to Balona.

MR. KUHL: I'm the one telling this story. You're supposed to sit quiet and listen. [Now Mr. Kuhl makes broad gestures with both arms.] But, lo and behold, Teddy rares up on his hind legs, like a mustang getting broke, and knocks that Green-Vest Man right off of his horse. And just then some lawmen come riding up, pick the fellow off of the ground, bid us farewell, and take him away. Can you believe all that?

TERY: I believe whatever you tell me, Mr. Kuhl.

MR. KUHL: [Smirks and sits back in his chair] Don't you ever believe everything a man tells you, child. You better learn that soon in life. I been telling you a tall tale. You never heard about tall tales?

TERY: [I lower my head, stare briefly at my lap, and must appear concerned, for at once Mr. Kuhl leans forward, his own expression now concerned.]

MR. KUHL: Oh, but everything *else* I been telling is the truth. It's only this latest part about the Green-Vest Man coming back and Teddy raring up is where I stretched it some. Stretched it considerable. I was telling you a Balona horse story there. We all tell 'em. Used to tell 'em.

∼

Kevin opens the door, peers in at us, raises his eyebrows. "No problem? Just noise? Okay." He leaves.

I decide we need to leave horse stories behind and get back to business. "And?" I say, cueing Mr. Kuhl. "What about some final problem? Could you review for that?"

"Grover got hisself a cold and coughed a lot, but everybody else was fine. Grover was always weak. Fast runner but weak. Mama always cottoned to him. Never gave me a hug. All my life, she never gave me a hug. 'Do something useful,' is what she would always say to me. She never said it to Grover."

Mr. Kuhl frowns as I pull up my stockings. "Finally you're fidgeting. You got to go?"

"I'm going to finish your story and turn it in. I'll be sure to see that you get a copy of the *Korndogger*. I'll bring it to you myself. It may be a week or so. And I'll bring along a sandwich."

"That'll be good. Remember the mayrnaise. So, okay. Knock-knock."

"Who's there?" I say.

"Well, I forgot already, but I know a better one. You know why the sailors can't play cards on their boat?'"

"Why's that?"

"The captain is sitting on the deck." Mr. Kuhl scratches behind his ear. "What was I just saying?"

"Sailors playing cards."

"Say, would you... before you go, would you give me a hug?"

It feels surprisingly appropriate to give Mr. Kuhl a hug as he sits forward in his chair, but leaning into him is awkward. He is trembling and his chest is heaving, as if he is trying not to breathe. He smells today like Grandpa's liniment.

After our brief hug, he sags back, deep into the chair.

"So I guess you're all done here. I guess you don't need to come no more." Mr. Kuhl's voice sounds as if he's being strangled. He seems suddenly weak and weary.

I want to respond with something chipper and encouraging, but all I can come up with is, "You've really been helpful, Mr. Kuhl. I can't thank you enough. I think yours is a great story."

He says, almost as a question, "You don't really have to come back."

I don't mention my plans to him, but I do intend to make more visits, now that we've become acquainted. To begin with, I'll bring him his sandwich and a copy of the *Korndogger.* As for now, we just look at each other and smile, as friends do when leaving each other for the moment.

Mr. Kuhl surprises me again, saying, "Shake, pardner." He holds his hand out to me, palm up. I extend my hand, and he takes it gently, holds it, squeezes. "You been into my heart," he says, "so, like it or not, you're gonna stay there." He drops my hand, turns away, waves me off with a grand gesture, like a prince dismissing me from his presence.

As I leave, Mr. Junior Kuhl appears to be trying again to see through that bush outside his window.

19

Reporter concludes her assigned journalistic tasks

Having submitted a disk each to Sheba and Mr. Peralta, as well as typed, double-spaced copies of my condensed version of Mr. Junior Kuhl's Great Earthquake history, I sit in the classroom considering the ambience. The odor is faintly that of damp dog and unwashed athletic sox. I waste a few minutes of leisure while waiting for Mr. Peralta's opinion. I rest my chin on my palm and peer through the streaky window at the high school lawn.

I can see where the recent merry graduates in their new gift cars have carved intersecting tire-track circles through the grass, a coming-of-age ceremony for half-wits, Daddy says.

Mr. Junior Kuhl was twelve when he arrived in Balona, not having a high opinion of automobiles. But I'm betting that by the time he became a successful eighteen-year-old businessman, and as the automobile market ballooned, his opinion would have changed considerably. I wonder if Mr. Kuhl had been one of those merry Balona grads long ago—or if not a grad, only merry.

Perhaps I'll make time to visit and try out some of those questions I didn't get around to asking him.

I'm sure that Daddy never engaged in destructive behavior like carving tire tracks in the school lawn, not only because he didn't have a car then, but because he has always carved mostly in stone. It occurs to me while contemplating the long brown lawn scars, that probably Daddy is busy carving Penny's initials in something. I wonder what Mommy thinks about that.

It now strikes me that for a very long time I have been unable to reconstruct Mommy's face in my mind. When she and I talk, I no longer see her; I seem only to hear her voice.

As Jack has reminded me several times, Mommy was the center of our family. She was the one who made the waffles and put medicine on our scratches and taught me how to knit. She played tennis with Daddy and she was a good swimmer. And there was nothing wrong with her. She always looked and acted like she felt great. And then, all of a sudden, there she was in her bed, groaning, with tubes going into and coming out of her. And then, practically right away, her ashes were in a niche out in Balona Cemetery, and Daddy was sitting in the living room with the drapes closed, staring at the carpet.

Her leaving like that hit all of us pretty hard. She was so lively and so pretty. And we were all so happy. Jack often reminds me, "she was such a good cook." His voice almost breaks when he mentions the *good cook* part. He says, "Of course, that was only about seven years ago, and already

I have a hard time remembering exactly what she looked like. Isn't that something?" So Jack suffers the same loss of vision. I wonder if Mr. Junior Kuhl can actually see his Poppy when he and Saneyor Kuhl converse.

Mr. Peralta is nodding his head over my story and *mmm-hmming* approvingly. Other staff members are still working on assignments, noses targeting their copy.

Sheba sits nearby painting her nails black, waving her fingers in the air from time to time. She says, "I'll get around to reading your story when my polish dries."

"This is excellent, Tery." Mr. Peralta speaks very quietly but I can tell that he is enthusiastic. "We'll start this at the top of the front page." He glances at Sheba. "Right, Sheba?" Sheba stops nail-painting and frowns fiercely.

Mr. Peralta explains, "We'll note that it's a contribution by cub reporter Tery Ordway and that it's been edited by Sheba Weiner." Sheba nods and resumes painting. "But it won't require any labor from you, Sheba." Sheba makes a satisfied face, eyes half-closed, one side of her black, or possibly green, lip up. "You'll need to reserve your creative energy for finishing your korndog-slaughter story before deadline." Sheba knits her brows. "But I'll work with you on that."

Sheba snorts, snaps her gum, blows on her fingernails, leans forward so that Mr. Junior Kuhl's silver locket swings forward from her neck, its dull sheen catching the light.

She looks me in the eye, sniffs, and gives me her one-sided smirk again. Even so, she doesn't look happy.

But Mr. Peralta stretches, nods, smiles contentedly.

"Well, everybody's right on track," he says. "We'll have a *Korndogger* that everyone can be proud of. Your contribution has helped a lot, Tery. Right, Sheba?"

"Yeah, yeah," she says.

Then she adds, "Even though I was ready to spike her story and had to keep on top of her all the time. Keep her from using too many big words and boring everybody with vocabulary and un-mature philosophy."

Sheba's constant negativity has caused me to modify my vocabulary, and that alone will surely make my story more endurable by lexically-challenged *Korndogger* readers.

I ask, "You don't need me to come back any more?"

"I guess not" replies Mr. Peralta. "Someday we'll get a new computer with more memory, and maybe that would speed the process. But for this issue we'll paste up and have the paper ready for Mr. Preene by the end of the week. Shouldn't take long to get printed. You have helped us in more ways than I can say, Tery. Maybe you'll consider being a correspondent, if we're somehow able to continue in the fall?"

Mr. Peralta says all this in a good loud voice, and several kids applaud. Tim nods in agreement. I lower my head modestly, shrug my shoulders in response to the question about continuing in the fall, say some goodbyes.

Tim has a nice smile for me. Although Tim is much older than I, and although I am not at all interested in romance, I think I'll sort of keep my eye on him.

"Have a nice day. Have a nice walk home," says Sheba, still finger-blowing. So I am not totally surprised to find that my bicycle has a flat again. Only one tire this time. At least Hopalong's spokes are not kicked out-of-true this time. Toe-tapping and coughing are not manifested.

∾

I have a dream that awakens me in the middle of the night, one of those dreams wherein reality mixes with fantasy, and it's difficult to tell whether you're awake or asleep. Sheba figures in my dream, sniffing and of course criticizing my vocabulary. Richie enters and begins strangling Sheba, not fatally, but enough so that her turning blue is satisfying to the dreamer. Sheba records the strangling as "live action" on her wrist phone. Weird.

Mr. Junior Kuhl's fine horse Teddy is a player, but only stands in the background, munching on a carrot. Daddy and Penny are there, wrapped in each other's arms, and Mr. Junior Kuhl's Daisy looks on, forbiddingly wagging her finger at Daddy. I am trying to capture the scene in a drawing, but the pencil lead keeps breaking.

I suppose the dream could represent frustration, but probably not, as I have completed what I set out to do. And I'm not at all frustrated. When I have become a psychiatrist, I will be able to interpret these things easily.

I'm not frustrated about the content of this dream. Irritated, perhaps, about the broken pencil. I don't like to be interrupted by unimportant events when I'm trying to concentrate.

Because of the warmth of the summer nights in Balona, I sleep with my window open. In the middle of the night, my weird dream begins to include unusual sounds, and I wake up hearing sirens. We have a loud siren atop the turkey factory out on the west side of town. That siren is used only for celebrations and floods and very large fire warnings. It is whooping vigorously. The volunteers' new engine has a traditional siren sound, not quite so loud, but also a horn that can waken the dead. I can hear it, also.

I lie in bed for a while, not really interested, until voices down in the street and car sounds, unusual for the middle of a Balona night, draw me up and to my second-floor, west-facing window. We don't have lots of street lights in

Balona, but the moon is bright, and I can see robed figures and some fully-dressed people coming out of their
houses and moving in groups east on First Avenue. The
very brightness of the moon creates a scene like out of
the old sci-fi movie, *Invasion of the Body-Snatchers*. Must
be a pretty big fire, I mutter, probably King Korndog
Inkorporated, a place subject to occasional blazes, hor-
rifying accidents, and the mysterious disappearances of
employees.

"You'd better see for yourself," says Mommy. And so I
dress quickly in sweats and tennies and join my family and
the crowds proceeding on foot.

We can see the glow of fire several blocks away, and I
get the feeling that Richie Kuhl has been out in the dark
of night exercising his power urges again. It may be that
King Korndog Inkorporated is in for smoke-damage reno-
vation, or worse.

20

Astonishing conclusion
to reporter's story

The fire is not consuming King Korndog after all. The fire
is at the Jolly Times Rest Home, and the building is fully
involved by the time we arrive. The staff has evidently
completed moving the residents away from immediate
danger, for there are occupied wheelchairs, walkers, and
folding chairs, lined up all along the sidewalk at a safe
distance across the street.

Kevin is draping residents in blankets, one of them
shrieking, "I want my own bed." Some are napping and
seem unaware of any problem.

Mr. Kon Chaud is smiling vacantly, intermittently clapping his hands. I scan for Mr. Junior Kuhl, but at first can
not find him.

The fire engine is parked at the hydrant in front of the
house next to the fire. All the searchlights are lit, and the

firemen are spraying the neighbor's roof, not the Jolly Times, with what looks like tons of water. There is a lot of noise, not only from the loud crackling fire itself, but from the firemen shouting, cursing—and laughing. Balona fires are always a production.

I can't help recalling Mr. Junior Kuhl's description of his own fire: "...yellow and blue flames shooting out...." Those are exactly the colors blasting from this fire.

"Why don't they try to put out the fire and save the building?" I am not the only one asking this question. But Daddy seems to know the habits of the brigade.

"It's already too far gone, Tery, so while they're waiting for the building to collapse, they're trying to keep the homes of neighbors from being damaged."

Brigade Captain Frank Floom is up on the engine, operating the water cannon. Searchlight Master Rowdy Brill, has one hand on his instrument that is trained on the stream of Captain Floom's water weapon. His other hand clutches a can of Valley Brew.

The crowd gasps at the height and beauty of the glistening silver arc as the water rises high over the roofs of the neighboring houses and into their backyards, possibly intended to wet typically wooden Balona fences.

Constable Cod Gosling, wearing white sweats that emphasize his bulk, is doing crowd control, mostly pushing kids back with one hand, alternately munching popcorn from a shopping bag clutched to his chest.

Daddy has his cameras working and is moving too close to the flames. Penny and Claire in their bathrobes stand gaping, grouped with other robed Balonans.

This fire has brought out a big crowd.

The blaze seems to be growing in intensity.

It is certainly emitting more heat.

At first trying to get as close as possible to the action, the eager viewers are now drawing back because of that increasing heat.

I catch a glimpse of Richie Kuhl.

Obviously not yet picked up by the sheriff's deputies, he is at one side of the crowd, in the front row of teen watchers alongside Pee Weiner, Sheba's little brother. Pee and Richie are both wearing black beanie caps and black sweats and small black backpacks.

They are laughing and high-fiving each other and jumping, their knees moving up and down in the manner of Irish line dancers. Pee is clutching his crotch like a small child needing to go to the bathroom.

Sheba in gray sweats and shower clogs appears at my side. "Almost didn't recognize you without your dumb red socks. See my man there?" She is not quite shouting in my ear. I wonder aloud at the large number of high school kids in the group of teens with Richie and Pee.

"Well, Richie like got out the crowd on his cellphone. Called me on my cellphone here." Sheba waves her wrist, phone attached. "Sort of person-to-person, told me I should write up a story about him for my paper. He like said it *your* paper, since he respects my professional. He meant the *Korndogger*, y'know." She leans in confidentially. "He went and discovered this fire, too, y'know, since he was like up and about, since he's a night-owl always looking for excitement."

"Is that so."

"Yeah. He's the one yelled 'fire' a few times in the street, he told me. I told him we like already put the *Korndogger* to bed, but he didn't understand my journalism-type lingo."

I finally get a clear view of Mr. Junior Kuhl.

He has moved all by himself into the street at the edge of the sidewalk across from the fire, a good forty yards from the flaming building, but much closer than most of the other Jolly Times refugees.

Mr. Kuhl is in his ankle-length blue robe. He is leaning, bent forward over his walker, as if to drink in the sight and sound and heat of the fire.

I push my way through the crowd, thinking that this huge conflagration must surely remind Mr. Kuhl of his tragic San Francisco fire. He is nodding his head and his lips are moving.

Mr. Carbunzle, big Kevin, and the rest of the Jolly Times staff are busy wheeling, pleading, pulling, leading the main body of old folks up the street toward the Balona High School gymnasium, where the residents are likely to be stashed until some decent housing might be found for them. I notice that Claire and Penny are helping there.

"Tery." My daddy's voice is distinctive, loud, and clear enough to be heard through the noise of any crowd. He is also gesturing for me to step back from the smoke and heat: "Get back here."

I wave in response, but I have already reached Mr. Junior Kuhl, standing next to him, hoping to persuade him to move back to safety.

I see at once that Mr. Kuhl's pale lavender aura has become purplish and its pink fizzles are more numerous.

He keeps repeating very clearly in a raspy voice, "Somebody got to do something. They're still in there." Tears are streaming down his face. "Nobody's gonna do nothing to save 'em. It ain't right."

I shout, "Is somebody still in there?" Mr. Kuhl isn't paying any attention to me. His gaze is riveted on the burning building.

212

Without warning, Mr. Junior Kuhl throws aside his walker and before I or anyone realize what he is about to do, and before anyone can stop him, and with neither hesitation nor limp, this 105-year-old man hikes up his robe and, white legs flashing gold in the firelight, scampers quick as a teenager across the street, over the lawn, toward the steps and the fiery entrance.

At that same moment a beam of black from the periphery catches my eye. More quickly than I have ever seen him move, Richie Kuhl races toward his great-grandfather, seemingly trying to intercept the old man before Mr. Junior Kuhl is able to reach the flames.

But Richie is too late. Richie's arm is outstretched and his fingers clawed, ready to grasp, but Mr. Junior Kuhl has already entered the doorway.

Junior Kuhl disappears into the blaze as the building collapses around him.

The pressure of the falling building throws Richie backwards, blow-back from the collapse of the building probably giving him some facial burns, but surely saving him from a flaming death.

Firefighters rush to drag Richie back to the street. Various of the spectators hoot, whistle, and applaud.

I stand gasping, my mouth wide open, too astonished to scream.

And too late to do anything but fail to stifle the multiple sobs that erupt despite my cool nature.

Was Richie really trying to save the old man?

Who knows what is truly in the heart of any person?

Epilogue

I am determined to be cool and mature, not wimp around. I am "maintaining an even strain," is how ex-marines Grandpa and Pastor Nim describe such an effort.

I have received many compliments about my piece on Mr. Junior Kuhl, not only about the condensed version in the *Korndogger*, but about the full-length series in the *Courier*.

Principal Croon has suggested to Daddy that it might be possible to fund a regular *Korndogger* beginning in the fall, as he has received many phone calls and personal remarks praising our efforts.

Publisher Mr. Preene suggests that I should think about writing a column for his *Courier*, the subjects of which might be at my discretion. Mr. Preene says that the Delta City *Beacon* wants to print my article on Mr. Junior Kuhl. So I have met my goal, done my "community service."

I plan to spend the rest of the summer helping Claire at her new cybercafé on Front Street, and playing tennis and riding Sal Shaw's horses and practicing aikido and reading and playing my piano and thinking about what I'll do for my classmates as their eighth-grade president in the fall. Penny has offered to give me some cooking lessons, and Senta says I'm long overdue for calculus. Sounds good. I'm also thinking about what subjects might make interesting newspaper columns.

I cannot let myself dwell on Mr. Junior Kuhl. Thinking about losing him tends to make me cry, and I don't cry very often.

After Daddy read my article that Mr. Peralta featured on the first and several other pages of the *Korndogger* he said, "You've been looking kind of grim lately, Babe. Gim'me a hug." And he grabbed me, hugged me so I was crushed against his chest, hugged me some more, and kissed me on the forehead, like he used to do once in a while before Penny showed up. That part is very good. "Hey, give me credit for knowing how it feels," he said.

I nodded and tried not to break into sobs. I knew right away he was talking about losing somebody you had become close to. We have learned that only one person died in that fire. No babies. Only one good old man.

Of course, I've been dreaming about Mr. Junior Kuhl. In my dreams he's alive and a lot younger and is worried that his mother doesn't love him. When I become a psychiatrist, I'll study stuff like that and maybe figure out why people waste time worrying about such trifles.

I suppose I must be immune to worries like that. I got to feeling close to Mr. Junior Kuhl, but I never got to actually loving him, the way maybe his grandson, Mr. Kenworth Kuhl, did. I am probably too cool even for that kind of love.

I say that because when I think about Mr. Junior Kuhl my eyes don't immediately fill with tears, the way Penny's eyes boil over when she thinks about Mr. Kuhl, or when she reads in the paper about somebody's pet being hit by a car. It's true that I sort of choke up a little, and I sigh a lot, but I don't cry. I've seen Jack cry when he plays the piano sometimes. I've seen Pastor Nim Chaud weep while he's praying. Not I. And I'm not gloomy all the time. Yes, I am probably too cool for most kinds of love. Nevertheless, I have the feeling that Mr. Junior Kuhl and I are going to stay in touch.

∼

It was Pastor Nim who decided that Mr. Junior Kuhl must have a memorial service for, as a man badly wounded in war and personally acquainted with grief, the pastor feels community needs. When I heard Pastor Nim's plans, Mr. Junior Kuhl's remark jumped to my mind, and I felt obligated to report his stated opinion of religion.

I said in a small voice, "'I think religion is bosh,' is what Mr. Kuhl said." Probably I should keep my mouth shut, instead of always trying to hint to people how much I know about things I don't really know anything about.

But Pastor Nim's surprising reply was, "Well, Tery, possibly much of it is bosh, at least to those who don't participate. But that doesn't mean a tasteful memorial service can't provide solace to survivors."

Then he gave me a task.

"Speaking of tasteful," he said, "the grapevine tells me that you sing Schubert. Maybe you could do us a song that Mr. Kuhl might have enjoyed?"

I was flattered. I knew the appropriate song, learned to sing it while accompanying myself. "I sing like a crow," I mentioned, hoping I sounded modest.

"Balona crows and I are members of Balona's Mutual Admiration Society," he said.

217

So, regardless of the soloist, a respectable number of people showed up and only a few show-offs. It was an almost entirely tasteful service.

After Pastor Nim delivered his tribute to Junior Kuhl, he called upon me, and I got up and sang "Du Bist die Ruh," accompaniment by Birdie Swainsler, Tabernacle's regular organist. The accompaniment swelled in all the right places, and although I don't yet have much muscle in my voice, at least I did the job in tune and didn't quaver too much.

Daddy looked proud. Somebody in back shouted "bravo" and started to applaud before the end, Balona style, but got shushed right away. Not so bad.

Probably more residents appeared out of respect for Pastor Nim than respect for Mr. Junior Kuhl, as Mr. Kuhl had reached such an age, and kept himself isolated for so long, that he had no contemporaries. Somebody passed around copies of the *Korndogger.* Pastor Nim read some lovely poems and scripture, and we all felt that wherever he is, Mr. Junior Kuhl must now be resting more easily than he did at the Jolly Times Rest Home.

That awful old place is a complete loss. It smoldered for several days, much to the frustration of the fire brigade.

Sheriff Anson Chaud says in a *Courier* interview that he has "personally investigated" and has declared that the fire at Jolly Times was "nobody's fault. Probably an electric problem, something like that."

There were no discernible indications of foul play, and the fire was so intense that Mr. Kuhl's remains may not be recoverable. "Nobody's fault there, either. Anyways, nobody died, so don't worry about it," the sheriff reported, obviously not recalling all the facts, as Balonans have come to expect.

Hannibal Chaud, Pastor Nim's father and our funeral director, announced at the memorial that a tablet will be erected in the Balona Cemetery, displaying Mr. Kuhl's dates and the legend that he was a "heroic pioneer of Balona." Mr. Kuhl will like the "heroic" part especially.

I'm convinced that Mr. Kuhl intended to save something or somebody when he ran into those flames. Perhaps he had his baby brother and sister in mind. Or Daisy. Or the gold watch with the green fob. And surely Poppy will be proud of him. Perhaps even his mother might have deigned to bestow a hug and a kiss on the forehead for his efforts.

Sheriff Chaud granted leave from the Chaud County Jail to his own sister, Mrs. Bapsie Kuhl, so she might attend the memorial for her grandfather-in-law. Mrs. Kuhl's sons sat between her and husband Kenworth Kuhl whose wife-wounded head was still arabesque in hospital bandages. Kenworth Kuhl wept audibly throughout the service.

Joseph sat looking straight ahead. Joseph and Kenworth were wearing coat-and-tie. Richie wore a T-shirt, kept giggling, whispering into his mother's ear. When not replying to Richie, Mrs. Bapsie Kuhl was craning her neck about, nodding and smiling.

Odd behavior at a memorial service, I thought, but maybe not for Mrs. Bapsie Kuhl. Richie also mugged for the cameras.

In the side aisle not ten feet from Richie crouched Mr. Blip Wufser, TV newsman from Delta City's KDC-TV. Mr. Wufser had brought a full complement of technicians with lights, cameras, and microphones, possibly catching every breath and burp in the sanctuary.

"Get that over here, not over there, and put that over here," Mr. Wufser would say in his resonant voice, and point at a piece of equipment for one of his minions to fetch or place. During the service he did this several times to the annoyance of all, almost shouting instructions, such as, "Get it on him, not him, on *him*." Mr. Wufser had cameras trained not on Pastor Nim, but on Richie, for it was Richie who had become the "Hero of Balona."

On whatever plane he now exists, Mr. Junior Kuhl would find that puzzling, if not ironic. Or perhaps he would find it encouraging.

At the end of the memorial for Mr. Junior Kuhl, Richie stood, turned, and showed his ruddy, fire-singed face to the congregation. He smirked, then bowed from the waist. Many in the congregation did applaud.

I have to admit that Richie's race toward the flames is puzzling. If I squeeze my eyes shut and stop breathing for a while, I can begin to entertain the remote possibility that he might have a good side. But then I revisit the sight of Richie bowing, then standing straight, facing the congregation, and displaying that terrible one-sided smirk.

For that is when I am reminded that over the heart of his dirty white T-shirt Richie had pinned a gold medal on a long red ribbon.

$\sim$

Sheba has called twice, confiding details of new abuse by her boyfriend. I find that worrisome, for she appears to have no one to turn to in crisis but a gossip-occupied mother. Inexperienced as I am, I could only listen, not offer advice. But as Sheba is very likely to be chief contender for *Korndogger* editor next fall, perhaps Mr. Peralta will provide counsel in an emergency. Sheba is sure to need it.

As far as anyone in Balona knows—or is willing to talk about—Richie has not been questioned about his suspicious activity at the Jolly Times fire. Nor has anyone else. The law expects and requires witnesses to step forward and testify in order to bring an evildoer to justice, but the witnesses need to offer more support than mere suspicion.

Pastor Nim in one of his sermons once mentioned a class of person, sometimes a person in public life, who is likely guilty, but is never apprehended, never pays for his crimes. Pastor Nim describes this person as "the eternally unpunished victor." Could that description be applied to Richie Kuhl?

Speaking of punishment and un-punishment, this morning we opened our Delta City *Beacon* to this news item:

Delta City—The California Highway Patrol reported today that a 17-year-old male motorcyclist suffered an accident early this morning on I-5. The cyclist is long suspected of being the daring black-clad highway vandal known to law enforcement as the Zorro Bandido who has "keyed" a number of moving vehicles on the Interstate.

According to big-rig driver A.J. Furd, 38, of Delta City, the close approach of the youth's headlight was clearly visible in Furd's rear-view mirrors. The alleged vandal apparently misjudged his distance from Furd's truck during the early hours today and bumped himself off the highway and into a bridge abutment.

When found unconscious on a bank of the Yulumne River, the young man was still clutching a 16-penny nail. He was not wearing a helmet. The name of the Balona youth was withheld because he is a minor. He is reported to be in critical condition in Doctors Hospital suffering from multiple fractures. Trucker Furd, owner of the vehicle the youth was allegedly attempting to vandalize, was not cited.

Who could that "Balona youth" be? We all know.

I do not wish disaster even for a criminal and a bully, especially for one whose recent motives and acts I still don't understand. Pastor Nim, a true optimist, often quotes the poet Robert Browning: "God's in His heaven, and all's right with the world." Maybe in Richie's case, Justice was only waiting to be served.

I have learned many things in the last couple of weeks about my family, about people in general and persons specifically, and about myself. And about death, as well as life. So, as I am both older and perhaps a bit wiser, I am now at least somewhat different from the person I was the day I met Mr. Junior Kuhl. And a better person? I hope so.

We haven't had any major aftershocks yet, but I am going to keep my consciousness tweaked for the possibility of meeting Mr. Junior Kuhl another time. And I will keep my "emergency bag" ready.

A mild aftershock
from Jonathan Pearce

It may be difficult to keep in mind while reading *Nobody's Fault* that both Tery and Junior are speaking as twelve-year-olds. Of course, Tery is awfully bright but, after all, she is a kid. And Junior Kuhl, ancient as he is in years, relates things that happened when he was "about twelve," so his recollections are those of a very young person, and thus most often are not expressed in fine language or sentences that will thrill an English teacher.

The great earthquake and fire that devastated San Francisco in 1906, can be only as real as the records that were kept to describe them. The descriptions in this book of the circumstances of the earthquake are as accurate as the available records will allow, tilted only very slightly to comport with the intentions of the characters.

The history of those events, along with what science has taught us about what can happen in and around a great earthquake, may also provide us today, a century later, with some stimulus to consider our own attitudes about preparedness for the next great quakes that are sure to batter our temblor-prone land.

BalonaBooks ®
http://www.balona.com